Tidal Kin

Lee Doty

Publisher Page
an imprint of Headline Books, Inc.
Terra Alta, WV

Tidal Kin

by Lee Doty

To order additional copies of this book or for book publishing information, or to contact the author:

Headline Books, Inc.
P.O. Box 52
Terra Alta, WV 26764
www.headlinebooks.com
Email: mybook@headlinebooks.com

Publisher Page is an imprint of Headline Books

ISBN 13: 9781946664150

Library of Congress Control Number: 2017953702

PRINTED IN THE UNITED STATES OF AMERICA

For Izzy, Helen and Ralph

1

Samoset Beach was crammed with well-oiled strangers lying inches apart under a turquoise sky. The cloying smell of sunscreen irritated Laney as she wove her way around beach umbrellas. The last hurricane had narrowed the beach, forcing her to tread carefully to avoid kicking sand on people's lunches.

She passed Red River Resort, a Victorian behemoth overlooking the salt marsh, the beach and Nantucket Sound. Gran told her it had been built by one of the captains who'd survived the Whaling Disaster of 1871. Judging by its odd, prow-shaped veranda, Gran figured the resort's main building stood in for the ship the captain had lost at sea.

At last she reached her spit of land. It looked like a bear's paw and was her favorite place to swim. She had a clear view of the lighthouse, the marsh, the resort, and Monomoy Island, but because of curves in the shoreline, no one could see her. Sunbathers never came out as far as the Paw, since they'd have to lug their chairs, coolers, and tents along.

With sweat trickling down her back—at thirteen, Laney kept her T-shirt on over her stubbornly flat chest—she rummaged through her backpack, slipped on water shoes, and raced into the waves. The ice-cold spray didn't faze her, and the seaweed entwining her legs reminded her of gummy worms, making her laugh.

For years Gran had forbidden her to come to the beach alone, but they'd finally reached a compromise. "If you take the lifesaving courses at camp, I'll let you go by yourself."

"You're the best, Gran!"

But the woman's pale green eyes had closed for an instant. "That is, when you turn thirteen."

When Laney's thirteenth summer finally arrived, Gran wasn't happy, but she'd made a deal and stuck to it.

Hopping on one foot, then the other, to shake water from her ears, Laney left the Paw and tucked herself beneath the nearby bluff. Gran had told her the bluff would eventually erode and provide a wider beach, but in doing so, would disappear. For now, Laney gratefully accepted its shelter from a strong wind.

She lay on her stomach and lined up her water shoes at eye level next to her towel. The flowery pink and orange shoes were the same ones worn by Isabella Miller, the most popular girl going into the ninth grade. To Laney's dismay, Gran had chosen the same style for herself, saying she and her granddaughter would look like twins at the beach.

Even though Laney had lived with Gran for five years, she still missed her mom. At first her longing had hurt so much she could only whisper about it to Bark, Aunt Norma's dog, who of course understood about missing a mother and allowed Laney to burrow into his furry neck. Laney knew why she'd been sent to live with Gran, but felt she was now old enough to care for herself and her mom. Gran would never agree to such a plan. Her mom's phone call from two years ago was enough to remind her why.

"I'm glad you answered the phone, Laney. This is just between us, baby. Promise me you won't tell Gran. You get your...things together. I need you. Promise you...won't tell."

"Okay, Mom. I promise. Are you coming here? You sound sleepy."

"I'm coming to get you."

Laney hadn't broken her promise. She hadn't told anyone about the call. She'd only asked Gran where her suitcase was.

Her mom didn't come that night and didn't call again for many months.

Laney's gaze followed a blue heron gliding low over the marsh, its stick legs dragging behind, marking a path through the gold-tipped grasses. Gran had taught her the names of plants and wildlife by the sea. Purplish beach plum and pink-flowering rosa rugosa now covered the bluff as far as she could see.

She reached for her summer reading book, but the heat made her too drowsy to read. She flipped onto her back and breathed in salty air. Her hands folded into the shape of binoculars and through them she studied the clouds. All around her waves heaved onto the beach with a crash, then skittered apologetically out to sea, only to come roaring back again.

Laney sprang upright. A burst of harsh words had startled her. Two men wearing long dark pants and white dress shirts stood in their bare feet at the end of the Paw. One shook his fist at the other, while the other blew cigarette smoke at the fist. Their words sounded foreign. She must have been sleeping when they first arrived, but no sooner had she reached that conclusion than she drifted off again. When she awoke for good, the men were gone. She'd been dreaming.

The beach crowd had now thinned as it was almost 5:00. Gran would be watching for her. She shook her towel and approached the water for a final rinse of her water shoes. A wave slapped a soggy cigarette pack against her leg. With echoes of Gran's environmental lectures in mind, she snatched it before the wave carried it off. The gold pack had red lettering—Golden Flake. She didn't recognize the brand, but she only knew her mother's.

"It's a lovely day, isn't it?" A tall man, hands caramel against his white cuffs, stood at the end of the Paw. Without waiting for her answer, he bent over to retrieve a pair of sandals. "How stupid of me to leave them here."

He sounded friendly, but something about him worried her. His formal clothes were out of place on the beach and his voice sounded foreign, convincing her she hadn't been dreaming about the men earlier.

He slipped on the sandals and buckled them.

She wanted him to leave but curiosity got the upper hand. "Where is the other man who was with you?"

"Oh. You've been here awhile? He left." The man smiled.

"Are you staying at one of the cottages?"

"You are full of questions, young lady. I'll ask you one. Have you been here all by yourself?"

Laney nodded, her face turning scarlet because she had no friends to meet at the beach.

The man shrugged. "I'm a loner, too." He scanned the beach, then the horizon. Finally he said, "Guess I'd better head home."

"Bye." She waved at his back before realizing how silly that was.

Laney needed to get home too but didn't want to follow him. A few more minutes couldn't matter. When the man had disappeared, she took a final look at the train of soft white clouds chugging along the horizon. An oblong object bobbing in the waves caught her attention. A seal? She knew better than to wade out too far, whether it was a seal or, even worse, a shark. There'd been three shark sightings already this year. She took several small steps closer.

At first she saw only the duct tape. She knew what that was because Gran had once wrapped her mother's broken tail light in it. But why would anyone put duct tape on a seal?

The waves rolled the object closer and she could see it more clearly now, but what she saw didn't make sense. A shirt? "No," she said aloud.

She stumbled backwards but couldn't look away. The object had a face. A man's face. He was staring at her. He kept staring at her. "No! No! No!"

2

Norma Bergen despised people who couldn't be troubled to take their emptied shopping carts to the cart return. If left to her, she'd shrink-wrap the offenders and toss them into their own carts like chicken breast.

She rolled an abandoned cart from the middle of a parking space to the nearby return, gave it a hard shove and walked back to lock her car. A shiny black BMW pulled in next to her, barely missing Norma's behind. Its driver was a heavy-set woman in a strapless sundress, wearing large, white-rimmed sunglasses and a small dog on her arm. Norma suspected the woman "summered" on the Cape, which was another thing Norma loathed—people who said they summered somewhere, as it implied wealth and a need to boast about it, to say nothing of the fact that such people turned an informative, concrete noun into an implication-soaked verb.

BMW lowered her window and aimed her flared nostrils, like twin bores of a shotgun, at Norma. "Maybe you didn't need to take two parking spaces."

Norma noted the sarcasm, another pet peeve. She responded, "Maybe if you lay off the fudge, *you* won't need two spaces."

She regretted having no time now for a parking lot fight, which normally guaranteed her forty-five minutes of oral argument. For a lawyer, what could beat that? Throughout her childhood, Norma had attended the Turn-the-Other-Cheek Club, until she discovered that that club, worldwide, had few members. She bought her groceries and hit the road.

Nothing could be less tempting than the stack of cupcakes on Norma's backseat. They were topped with blobs of red, white and blue frosting, perfect for a Wheezy Wickersham Fourth of July party. She had to amend her earlier thought. One thing was less tempting than the cupcakes—it was Wheezy Wickersham's party, especially as it fell on the first day of Norma's annual two-week Cape staycation.

Visitors over the years had said it must be wonderful living on Cape Cod, yet Norma rarely had a chance to enjoy it. Her days were filled with office work, errands, bill-paying, and all the other things people do who live in Birmingham, Boise, and Buffalo. To solve the conflict of living the life of a drone, in the old-fashioned sense, and living it in paradise, she carved two weeks out of each year during which she pretended to be a tourist enjoying the Cape—swimming at dawn with her dog, Bark, sailing on the bay with Anne and Anne's granddaughter, Laney, even dining on the day's catch, in her bathtub, alone. How Norma hated Wheezy's parties for keeping her from all that.

"This is the problem," she'd confided to Anne, who'd also received an invitation. They stood side by side at the transfer station, tossing huge trash bags into a foul-smelling chamber. "I don't like Wheezy. I don't like her perfect lawn. Did you see how they planted it? Looked like hair plugs. And speaking of hair plugs, I don't like that bald stick of butter she married and I especially don't like her name. Wheezy. Why would anyone refer to herself as chest congestion?"

One last hoist and the women moved to the recycle area.

"What's the big deal, Norm? Just don't go."

Anne had separated her newspapers from cardboard, wine bottles from water bottles, milk cartons from egg cartons, all of which Norma saw as hair-splitting. "I can't 'not go.' I've missed the last two parties and if I don't go this time, she'll jump out from behind my hedge and ask in that whiney voice of hers, 'What's wrong? I thought we were friends.' She'll want to understand why I don't like her and how she can improve our relationship. I'm tempted to tell her."

"Norm, you're a fraud. You're going to the party because you don't want to hurt her feelings."

Norma hoped Anne was wrong. This was no time to go soft.

Anne and Norma were the only year-rounders nearby. Both single, they occupied cottages on either side at the top of Samoset Bluff Lane, a short dirt road through a scrub pine forest that ended down by the beach. Their grey shingled capes were like wounded soldiers holding out against the forces of wealthy retirees, all ready to stampede the last two tear-downs with a water view.

The cottages were about the only thing the women had in common. Anne was creative, poised and refined. For years she'd taught piano at the Curtis Institute of Music, and had retired at sixty to raise Laney on the Cape. Anne's parents had left her the cottage years before, and as she'd told Norma, the location was far enough removed from her daughter, Gin, Laney's mother, to assure the young girl some stability.

A credential like Curtis accounted for little with Norma. It was Anne's ability to play anything she heard by ear, instantly and movingly, that so astounded her. Nothing soothed Norma's prickly soul as much as Gershwin descending the bluff on a summer breeze.

Norma turned off Route 28 and thought back to when she'd met Anne for the first time. It was a windy Saturday in November and Main Street's trees were bare. Norma recognized her new full-time neighbor when, rounding the corner at the hardware store, they nearly collided.

"I'm not sure whether this drill bit is the right size." Anne held one bit and then another, explaining to Norma her bookshelf project as though the two had known each other for some time. "I don't want to have to drive all the way back here if I'm wrong on size."

Norma had been making her own household repairs for twenty years, ever since, a year out of law school, she'd chucked her job at a large Boston firm and bought her cottage, long abandoned but gamely described by her realtor as "rough and ready."

While Anne considered drill bits, Norma studied her neighbor's delicate features: soft, shoulder-length blond hair streaked with gray, and long, tapered fingers. Rumor had it that Anne had suffered bad luck—early widowhood, troubled offspring—but she showed no signs of self-pity or that worse thing, nonstop talking. Norma made a decision.

"Leave the bits. I've got a shop in my storage shed. No tool I don't have, no repair I haven't made."

Despite being twenty years her junior, Norma enjoyed spending time with Anne. It was a new experience for her, friendship.

Norma flipped on her blinker and pulled in close to her mailbox, nearly clipping a man rushing by on foot. The man was wearing a tie, unusual for the Cape, and didn't turn when Norma yelled, "Watch it, Brooks Brothers."

She'd spent years stopping by the post office for mail on her way to her office, but now that she'd converted her dining room to a home office, a large mailbox at the top of the bluff made more sense. She reached inside and pulled out a thick business envelope that had been stuffed toward the back. It was crumpled and might have sat for a few days. She pulled into her driveway and opened it.

Summons and Complaint

"Who the hell is suing me?"

3

Normally Anne took great pleasure in running her fingers along her porcelain-encased desk clock, but now it was telling her Laney was late. She'd spent the afternoon paying bills and preparing macaroni salad for Wheezy's party, but had eaten as many olives as she'd dropped into the salad, leaving her feeling queasy. Or maybe the cause was resentment at paying Gin $1,800 a month to stay away from Laney. Anne thought of all the things she could have done for Laney with extra money—travel, private school, tennis. As musicians, she and Gordon had never made much money, and the annuity she'd bought with his life insurance proceeds was hardly generous. *Gin.*

Anne had missed Gordon at first. His unassuming presence had been part of her scenery for thirty years. Sometimes, when he'd played his cello, his heavy eyelids and long, sad face reminded her of a Nubian goat. A few years into widowhood forced her to admit that Gordon's main attraction had been his passivity. He wasn't bothered that she made the important decisions in the household, like where they lived, how they spent money, even which musical engagements they accepted. In fact, she'd made all the decisions except those concerning their daughter. Gordon had named her Virginia after his own mother. Gin abhorred her name, especially as a rebellious teenager, when she started spelling it without the final I, to make it sound like vagina. They'd reached a compromise with Gin.

In Gordon's eyes, Gin was perfect and he discouraged Anne from interfering in her upbringing. As Anne had never wanted a child, and only yielded to Gordon's desire for one in return for his agreeing to end the sexual side of their marriage, she was happy to oblige him. If he could see his daughter now, how would Gordon rate the job he'd done raising dear Virginia?

She checked the time again. 5:30. Norma was also due any minute, as they'd planned to go to Wheezy's together. Norma had taken Laney to the ball game the night before and kept her overnight, and Anne wanted to remember to thank her. She left her study and headed upstairs to change for the party. If Laney still hadn't shown when she came down, she'd go looking for her.

Norma flung open Anne's front door. "For God's sake, Anne, are you here?" Her voice boomed throughout the cottage. Norma always made a startling entrance, whether she was in full crisis or borrowing a cup of sugar.

Anne, dressed in an ivory cotton skirt and matching shell blouse, met her in the living room. "Norm, are you sure you want to go to the party in a T-shirt that says 'Bite me'?"

She was teasing. Anne would never try to make Norma conform to fashion standards. If Norma wanted to keep her beauty a secret, that was her business. Anne looked at her now. Despite searing blue eyes and full, shapely lips, Norma's allure was obliterated by hunched posture, duck-footedness, and a complete rejection of feminine style. Norma's idea of haute couture was the Bite Me shirt, baggy jeans, and a bucket-shaped fishing hat in which she stuffed her long, thick, sun-bleached hair.

Even beyond appearance, Anne would never want to change her friend. One of Norma's unusual traits was that she had the gumption to say things that needed saying, even if she knew them to be untrue, like that time several years ago when they'd tried to register Laney for third grade.

Her granddaughter had arrived on the Cape with bad memories and a distracting facial tic, frantic blinking that surfaced whenever she was nervous. Anne had tried to calm her before the registration meeting with the principal, and had asked Norma to come with them, as her antics usually lightened the mood all around. By the time they reached the school parking lot, however, Laney's eyes were flashing S.O.S. in Morse code.

They sat, three in a row, knees touching the principal's desk, with Laney between Anne and Norma. There wasn't a sheet of paper or photo or flower or anything on the desk other than a nameplate: Melody Fluck, Principal.

Ms. Fluck remained stiff and silent while Anne introduced Laney, explained that Norma was Laney's godmother, and filled in the gaps of Laney's sparse educational history. As she spoke, she couldn't help noting Ms. Fluck's unusually long torso and neck. Coupled with eyes set far apart, the principal's resemblance to a giraffe was too obvious for anyone, particularly elementary school children, to miss. On top of that, she had a naughty-sounding surname, leaving her prey to childhood mischief and adult pity. All this Anne concluded after the meeting. During the meeting, she could only wonder where the woman's insensitivity came from.

"And Laney's first and middle name? Is it really Alanis Morissette? Perhaps you could explain that, Ms. Sager."

Anne also thought it outrageous that Gin had named her daughter after a rock singer, especially one whose award-winning album, "Jagged Little Pill," summoned up the nightmare of Gin's own life of addiction. In front of Laney she could only squeeze out a meek smile and say, "A phase of her mother's."

"Well, I would have expected you to have had more influence in such a critical matter. That you didn't probably explains a great deal. But let me save us all some valuable time. You don't need to waste yours filling out forms for the third grade and I won't waste mine reviewing them. Based upon her poor school attendance alone, your granddaughter will have to be retained in second grade. If that doesn't suit you, there's always private school. Now, anything else?" Ms. Fluck pressed her hands against her desk as if to rise.

Anne knew Laney was bright. She also knew the embarrassment of having to repeat second grade would be worse for Laney than having to work hard to catch up to grade level. Didn't every educator know that? Anne pleaded Laney's case, and the more she did, the more sanctimonious Ms. Fluck's responses became. But when Ms. Fluck turned to Laney and asked her to "stop that blinking," Norma took over.

"Excuse me, Ms. Fluck. Laney, would you mind stepping outside for a moment?"

Only when the door closed did Norma continue. "What's the matter, Melody? You don't like kids? Or maybe there are just certain ones you don't like. Are you bothered by the possibility Laney has Tourette syndrome—might disrupt the class? The fact that you're not even willing to evaluate her suggests you might be. Do we need to take the matter up with the superintendent in a Section 136A filing?"

Preparing to do battle, Ms. Fluck seemed to further elongate her neck. "I don't know what you're talking about."

Norma stood. "I think you do. And the super does too. He won't appreciate yet another 136A when he's on his way to Boston to plead for funds."

Anne was on the verge of saying Laney didn't have Tourette syndrome when Norma cut her off. "Don't! Don't say another word, Anne. I can tell you're upset."

Norma rolled out more code references, case citations, and potential grim outcomes for Melody Fluck if she didn't do what she was "legally obligated to do." She bombarded the principal with erudite legislative history, fiery administrative law rulings, and astronomic fines and penalties should Fluck be found in violation of the law. By the time they left Fluck's office, Laney was enrolled in the third grade and Anne had learned the value of letting Norma be herself. She also learned about Section 136A.

"What is that anyway, Norm?"

"Not sure. I think it came up in a dangerous dog case I handled."

Now, the image of defeat, Norma sat slumped against Anne's couch, eyes closed, moaning. "God. God."

"Need a glass of something?" Anne asked.

"Scotch."

When Anne returned with the drink, Norma was staring at the ceiling. Without a word she took the glass and swallowed the liquid.

"Tell me what's up, Norm."

"You won't believe what those scumbags did."

"Which scumbags?" Anne sat down and stole a glance at her wristwatch.

"The bozos who now own the Inn at Cockle Cove. I used to represent this nice old lady, Mary Temple, when she owned the inn. She willed it to her sons, the bozos. You knew Mary— short silver hair with bangs, leathery skin, always a big smile? Now her sons are planning to sue me. They've sent me a copy of the suit papers, demanding I have my insurance company contact them or they'll actually file the suit."

"What's their claim?"

"Their mother owned the inn, but she also was in partnership with the owners of Red River Resort. She decided to sell her Red River interest to the other Red River partners so she'd have capital to put into Cockle Cove Inn, make some renovations before she died. I did the legal work. Her sons now say Mary needed their consent to sell her interest in Red River. They say she'd given them a right of first refusal, in writing, and claim I knew about it and ignored it, or worse, persuaded Mary to ignore it. Assholes."

"When was the sale?"

"About eighteen months ago."

"Why didn't they speak up then?"

"Good question. They don't live here and they say they didn't know about the sale until their mother died. They say their mother must have forgotten about needing their consent because she was mentally incapacitated, and I should have known that she wasn't capable of handling her own affairs. It's such bullshit."

Norma shook the ice cubes in her glass and poured them into her mouth. Anne almost had to raise her voice over the savage crunching. "Sounds fishy to me, Norma. What do they want you to do about it now?"

Norma didn't answer.

Anne had never seen her friend so pale. "Norma?"

"They want a lot of money for my alleged negligence. Millions."

In the distance a siren wailed, almost like a sound effect for the disastrous sum.

"Ridiculous. They're just being greedy. The jury will see they're gold-digging." Anne tried to think of other reassuring comments. "Can you just turn it over to your insurance company and let them handle it?"

Norma's shoulders sagged. "I've had to cut back on expenses. Haven't paid my premium. Bastards!" She held out her glass for a refill.

The epithet seemed to embrace Mary Temple's sons as well as the insurance company. Anne wished she could spend more time helping Norma, but she was concerned about Laney, normally punctual to a fault and now an hour overdue. Was that siren getting louder? "I'll get your drink and then I'm just going to shoot down to the beach. Laney's late." As she stood to go, Laney called from the front yard.

"Gran! Open the door. My hands are full."

"I'm relieved she's back, but I'm going to talk to her about making me worry," Anne said as she opened the door. "What in the world?" A uniformed officer stood behind Laney.

"Somebody drowned, Gran." Laney dropped her gear in the front hall. She spotted Norma in the next room and ran in. "I found a man, dead. It was awful. *I* found him."

4

Norma took in Laney's state. The girl rocked from side to side trying to get her story out, but her chattering teeth made it impossible.

Anne thanked the officer, grabbed a throw from the couch, and wrapped it around Laney's shoulders. "Don't talk." She rubbed her shoulders and shushed her. "Norma, will you make some tea while we get dry clothes?"

"But we have to go back to the beach, Gran. The police say they need me to tell them what happened and you have to go with me."

"Hold the phone." Norma stood. "What do you mean by 'what happened'? How would you know? Did you see the man drown? Who's down there saying you need to make a statement, Laney? Barney Fife?"

"*Norm.* Don't grill her."

"Oh come on, Anne. Everyone knows the locals should always defer to the state troopers when there's a death like this."

"Just go easy."

When Norma returned with the tea she said, "But what did you see, Laney? Why do the police want you to come back?"

Laney's tic, almost outgrown, came back with a vengeance as she tried to tell her story. "I was getting ready to walk home from the Paw—that's what I call the end of the beach."

"What? Why were you all the way down there?" Anne's voice was shrill.

Norma said, "Who's grilling now? Go on, Laney."

19

"I'm not sure what happened next." The girl closed her eyes. "I must have cried out or something because this lady came up to me and asked what was wrong and then she started screaming and then there was a big crowd and then this police in regular clothes.... I just can't remember anything else."

"I'm putting brandy in the tea, Anne. Don't argue with me."

The women plied their charge with laced tea and peanut butter sandwiches. They kept conversation general until Anne took Laney upstairs.

Norma mulled over Laney's situation as she finally got around to her scotch refill. Much as she was annoyed about the questioning Laney was bound to undergo with the police, the girl was unharmed and her scary story might even give her a certain cachet when school started. But having reassured herself about Laney, she'd only freed herself to fret about her own problems.

In her brief glance at the Summons and Complaint, she'd seen references to an agreement that described Mary Temple's legal obligations to her sons in the event she sold her interest in Red River Resort. In conducting her due diligence, a review of background documents to make sure the sale was proper, Norma would have come across those legal obligations. So why did she have no memory of them? "Because they didn't exist, that's why," she told herself.

And how about the buyers, the other partners owning Red River Resort? Why weren't they being sued too? They had deep pockets, right?

She brooded over these questions as she took her empty glass to the kitchen. Through the window above the sink she could see Wheezy and her party friends gathered along Anne's split-rail fence. They were all watching a man clearly headed for Anne's front door. Tall, mid-forties, heavy brow over dark eyes, khaki shorts, and a faded blue baseball cap. Nice enough looking. Familiar too. Norma wondered if he was the "police in regular clothes" who'd shown up when Laney discovered the body. He came down the stone path.

"Ugh." She took her time reaching the screen door, despite his repeated knocks on the door frame. "Keep your shirt on. I can hear you." She opened the door and yelled, "Go away!" in the general direction of Wheezy's crowd, and let him in.

The man, removing his cap, looked at her in surprise. "Hello. I didn't expect *you* to be here."

"Who the hell are you?"

"Sorry." He smiled. "I thought you might remember me. I recognize you from the Baxter case. You're Norma Bergen? You handled the defense very well. I was a witness for the prosecution."

"Right." It pissed her off he was bringing up a case she'd lost. It was probably a deliberate ploy to put her on the defensive. "Anyway, you'll have to remind me of your name."

He nodded and said, "Let's start again. I'm Lieutenant Will Coigne, a state trooper. We investigate—"

"I know. You investigate serious crime. You work out of the State Police Barracks in Skaket and report to the District Attorney. Established in 1869, Massachusetts has the oldest state police force in the northern hemisphere. So, now that we've settled that, what do you have to do with an accidental drowning?"

"May I come in?" His eyes were still smiling, but they held questions too.

She stepped back. By now she remembered him, and what she'd learned about him during the Baxter trial. He was tied to the Irish Mafia—at least his father was for certain, and word had it he was too. His father was now serving time for crimes of the heinous variety. No way that kind of thing didn't rub off on a son. Nothing sickened Norma like a dirty cop. How he ever got to be a state trooper, much less a lieutenant, she didn't know.

"It's really a coincidence that I was in the area when the call came in about the drowning victim. I've been staying—"

"Let me help you get to the point, Coigne. You want to speak with Laney because you think a thirteen-year-old has unique insights about some poor guy who had the bad taste to drown on the Fourth of July. You want to talk to her even though the beach was full of adults who saw the same damn thing."

For a second he looked surprised, then he recovered, but without his smile. "Would you ask her to come here, please?

I understand the young lady lives with"—he referred to his notes—"her grandmother, Anne Sager?"

"The *child* is in shock, Lieutenant and won't be available for some time. When she is, we'll have her write down what she knows. I'll make sure you see it. Fair enough?"

Still standing by the front door, Norma noticed a Ford Taurus unmarked cruiser idling by the fence.

Coigne said, "I'd like to speak to Ms. Sager too. Now."

She hadn't expected pushback. Was this guy just looking for something to do on a hot afternoon, or was there more to the drowning than she thought? Something in Coigne's tone worried her. She kept her hand on the doorknob and studied his face. Officer Friendly had disappeared. In his place was a man confident he knew more about the facts of the drowning than she did.

"What's up, Coigne? Why can't this wait? And what's the cruiser for?"

It was Coigne's turn to make an assessment. She knew he was trying to figure out whether he'd get more cooperation from her if he opened up or not.

"We need to have the girl come to the Barracks. The situation is more complicated than a drowned guy with poor taste."

"Okay, I wasn't respectful—"

"It's unlikely the death was accidental, unless the guy was trying to see how long he could hold his breath with his mouth, hands, and feet bound. If that was the case, then I guess you could call it accidental. Obviously we'll draw no conclusions one way or the other until we investigate."

For a moment neither spoke. Then Norma asked, "Do you know who it was?"

"Not yet. Doesn't look like a tourist though."

"Why do you say that?"

"No bathing suit, fully clothed, ready for business."

Norma wanted to keep the questions rolling to forestall his interview with Laney. It wasn't just that the girl had had a shock. Norma didn't want Coigne poking around in her past, which was bound to come out. Having to talk about her worthless mother and absent father would only upset her.

"Don't be close-minded, Lieutenant. He could be a tourist. He parks the wife and kids in a cottage down here for two weeks and comes out from Boston to see them on the weekend."

"Don't think so. Guy like that takes off his tie soon as he crosses the bridge. Not this man."

"Bound with his own tie? Efficient."

"Look, I'd like to stick around and hypothesize, but I'm actually a little busy."

Sarcasm, second time in one afternoon. How she hated it. "Didn't think you state troopers knew words like hypothesize."

"You going to go get them or do I have to?"

Before she could answer, Laney and Anne were on their way downstairs. Laney had regained some color and lost her wide-eyed look, but Norma still worried. If the drowning victim had met with foul play, then word of the highly visible visit by the police would spread, possibly to the perpetrator, putting Laney in harm's way. Maybe she was overreacting, but Norma wanted control of the interview and wanted it brief.

"Anne, Lieutenant Coigne here wants to talk to Laney about—"

"She won't be gone more than an hour, Ms. Sager."

"*Gone*?" Anne stared at Coigne. "You want to take her somewhere?" Anne turned to Norma. "Can't they talk here? She's had a shock."

"It looks as though it wasn't an accidental drowning, Anne." Norma walked over and held both Lancy's hands. "The man who drowned was tied up with his tie, so they figure someone intended him to drown."

Coigne's voice rose. "You need to let *me* handle this witness."

Anne moved between Laney and Coigne. "She's not a witness, Lieutenant. She's an eighth grader going into ninth."

"It wasn't his tie, Aunt Norma. It was tape. Duct tape."

5

Laney felt proud to share information even Aunt Norma didn't have.

Lieutenant Coigne was the first to break the silence that followed her announcement. "What else do you remember, Laney?"

"She already told us she remembers nothing."

Aunt Norma sounded mad. Laney wondered if she was signaling for her to keep quiet. For her own reasons Laney hesitated to tell Lieutenant Coigne about something she'd just remembered: the foreign man who returned for his sandals. What if the police put him in jail because of her? He'd be furious, at *her*. Besides, she didn't get a good look at him, just his sandals. And that other man with him, was he even real? The police would think she imagined them both and they'd be unhappy with her too.

Raised voices brought her back to the present.

"She's going to have to come with me, Ms. Sager. Maybe she'll recognize someone from a photograph."

"That's preposterous." Aunt Norma smacked the side table, jostling Gran's favorite lamp, its base a glass jar with a miniature ship inside. "Are you suggesting the killer hung around to watch the tide roll his victim in and Laney might have spotted him?"

Aunt Norma's outburst shocked everyone, especially Laney, who only then realized that Sandal Man, as she now thought of him, might have something to do with the drowned man's death.

"Enough, everyone. This is all more than I can handle, let alone a thirteen-year-old. Lieutenant Coigne, Norma will give you a call to arrange something."

"You understand, Ms. Sager, every second we delay could mean the difference between a quick arrest and a cold case, possibly other deaths."

Other deaths! Laney felt scared and stupid. If only she were someone like Isabella Miller, who would know exactly what to do. And she'd be brave about it. Laney's eyes blurred with tears and her throat began to ache.

A soft knock at the front door cut off further talk and Gran excused herself.

"I'm sorry we couldn't get to your party, Wheezy. We're rather tied up—"

"Oh no, forget it, Anne." Mrs. Wickersham barged past Gran into the living room. "We're just concerned, that's all."

Her pitched eyebrows made Mrs. Wickersham look concerned, but Laney knew this neighbor well. She probably wanted to meet Lieutenant Coigne, find out what was going on, and get in the middle of it. Laney wondered if all the neighbors knew about the dead body on the beach.

Gran only managed to back her neighbor out the door by accompanying her. Meanwhile, Aunt Norma picked up her argument with Lieutenant Coigne.

"Tomorrow morning. It's more cost-effective that way. By then, you'll know the victim's identity and have a smaller universe of suspects for her to look at. You may even have your man, or woman, in custody."

"Aunt Norma? I need to ask you about something."

"Just a minute, Laney. Let's be efficient, Coigne. We'll get her there tomorrow *if* you still need her."

Using Gran's strategy for removing unwanted guests, Aunt Norma escorted Lieutenant Coigne outside. "Back in a sec, kid."

Laney gathered her gear and hung her backpack in the closet. Gran called it a cloak room because it had hooks and cubby holes and was large enough to walk in. She stuck her damp towel next door in the laundry closet.

She knew why Gran was opposed to her being questioned at a police station. The last time they'd been to one, years ago, Laney had hit a woman in the face and made her cry.

The memory always brought back that same helpless terror. She'd sat on a wooden bench in a large, windowless room with torn carpet and pale green walls—at least the harsh lighting made the walls look green. Her back against the wall, she got to watch the parade of people trudge by, some yelling, some crying, some filthy, and some who walked as though they'd wet their pants because their legs were chained together.

A woman waited beside her. She'd visited their apartment sometimes. Laney remembered her black rubber shoes shaped like small bread loaves. Her mother used to get angry whenever the woman wrote things down in her notebook.

The police had taken her mom across the room behind a gray partition. The far wall was lined with many partitioned cubicles, but Laney was able to keep track of her mom by locating her candy cane socks showing in the gap between the floor and the bottom of the partition.

Whenever her mom was in trouble, the routine was for Gran to show up at the police station and the three of them to return to the apartment. Laney would be sent to bed with a peppermint treat from Gran. In the next room, Gran would make hissing sounds and her mom would cry, and Laney would finally drift off.

Laney was relieved when Gran finally arrived. She stood to go, but Gran asked her to wait while she spoke privately down the hall to the woman with the rubber shoes.

When they returned, Gran did not look at her. "Button up, sweetheart. It's time to go."

"What about Mommy?"

"She's not coming right now, Laney."

"I have to wait for her."

"She's already left."

"No she did not. I see her socks." Laney pointed.

Gran lifted her up anyway.

"Gran, we have to wait!"

Laney screamed and twisted and kicked in Gran's arms. When the rubber-shoes woman tried to calm her, Laney hit her hard in the nose.

For a long time Laney believed it was because she'd hit the woman that her mom was sent to jail. Now, all she knew was that she didn't want to go to a police station ever again. She resolved to say nothing to Aunt Norma, the police, or anyone else about Sandal Man. She would remember nothing.

The front door closed and Gran and Aunt Norma returned to the living room. Gran was shaking her head, but also smiling a little. "I'm not sure calling her Wheeze-Bag was helpful, Norma."

Soon Aunt Norma left to get some work done and look after Bark, who was afraid of fireworks. Laney and Gran ordered pizza and walked a mile to a neighboring beach because their own was still blocked off by the police.

The events of the day were forgotten amidst eardrum-shattering sky bursts of diamonds, rubies, and emeralds, but any relief from the day's tension was short-lived. A bandaged tail light in the driveway announced an unexpected visitor.

6

Since she rarely locked her doors on the Cape, Anne assumed her daughter let herself in, fixed a drink, and was now rifling through Anne's desk or handbag.

"Mom's here! Do you think the police called her? She must have been worried about me."

Anne closed her eyes. For Laney to believe that Gin's arrival had anything to do with concern for her was almost comical and sad.

Anne reached over and tugged her ponytail. "Let's find out what's up." Her hand brushed Laney's earlobe, reminding her of her granddaughter's campaign to get her ears pierced. When she was a teen, Gin hadn't even asked. She'd had every piece of loose flesh, including her tongue, pierced at least once. For a fraction of a second Anne had been tempted not to take her to the doctor when her tongue became infected, but she'd relented. Gordon hadn't been dead a month and some acting out was to be expected. That's what Gin's therapist had said, month after month.

The house was quiet as they entered. Anne looked for the usual trail of Gin's belongings, dropped like little breadcrumbs in the forest. Instead, the living room was as they'd left it, with the exception of a well-dressed couple seated on the couch, holding hands, eager faces turned to greet them.

The man unfolded to a height of over six feet.

"Mom!" Laney rushed forward.

"That's my baby." Gin stood and offered Laney a cheek.

The interlude gave Anne a chance to take a good look at her. *Clean hair and nails? Matching handbag and sandals? Silver necklace with a shark charm—how fitting. But I must be dreaming. Gin looks like a model for Lilly Pulitzer.* Anne turned toward the man. "Who's our company, Gin?"

Gin extricated herself from Laney's hug and grabbed the man's hand. "I can't believe you don't recognize your own chamber of commerce president. Isn't Red River about the smallest town on earth?"

"Ken Crawford, Ms. Sager." The man shook Anne's hand.

He looked familiar. In Anne's experience, everyone on the Cape resembled everyone else, especially in the summer, but Mr. Crawford looked more cosmopolitan than most Cape Cod year-rounders. He was trim and tan, and had intelligent, dark brown eyes. His face was smooth, braced by some barely detectable, musky aftershave. But he wasn't perfect. When he smiled, Anne noticed his clear dental retainer.

"Mom! Did you hear about the drowning?" Laney looked like she'd burst if she couldn't tell the story.

"Is that what you were telling me about, Kenny? The man they found on Samoset Beach?"

Laney launched into an embellished rendition of her discovery on the beach until Anne steered them toward lighter topics, such as Gin's long drive from Philadelphia and the worsening summer traffic on the Cape. Crawford volunteered that he was one of the owners of Red River Resort, and they discussed the magnificent views from its veranda.

Anne figured she'd let Gin choose the moment to explain her reason for breaking the rule, never to show up uninvited. The explanation was imminent. Gin's fingers twirled a lock of hair. The "tell" always preceded a disastrous announcement: "I've been expelled, I'm pregnant, I've been arrested."

Anne glanced at Laney, whose eyes were glued to her mother. She could only be described as enraptured.

"I may as well spit it out. Mother, Kenny and I are getting married. We're here to get Laney."

In the silence that followed Anne almost did the unthinkable, laughed. Marriage? Her infantile daughter? Then again, she should have foreseen the day when Gin would find another funding source, one that didn't require work in the conventional sense, of course. But Gin's announcement about taking Laney was no laughing matter.

In the near distance someone set off firecrackers. It sounded like the last few kernels of corn popping in a microwave. Anne kept her voice even. "Laney's had a long day. We'll talk about your news in the morning."

"I want to stay up, Gran."

"Your grandmother's right, Laney." Crawford rose and put his arm around Gin's waist. "We're not used to a girl's schedule yet. We'll come back in the morning." He nodded at Gin, then Anne, as though he'd deftly resolved a brewing conflict at the chamber.

Anne was worried. She had no legal right to keep Laney, having only persuaded Gin to leave her on the Cape by baldly offering an "allowance." Gin would always be a selfish, neglectful parent, and for that reason alone custody of Laney was out of the question. But what also struck Anne at that moment was that she couldn't imagine her own life without Laney. The child offered her something she needed. A second chance to get it right? She wondered.

"Better yet, we'll take you both to breakfast at Red River Resort. We can dialogue, make a plan that meets everyone's goals."

"Good idea, Kenny. I'm staying at the resort, Mother, but we'll pick you up in Kenny's car. Wait until you see it. It's time my Laney saw a little of the good life." Gin shifted her Kate Spade handbag on her shoulder. She was about to head out when Crawford cupped her elbow and gently guided her toward Laney. Gin air-kissed her daughter and squeezed her shoulder.

"See you in the morning, hon. Wear something special."

Anne shut the door behind them and leaned back against it. This was not the first time she'd had to fight for Laney and it looked like she'd have to do it again.

Laney was far too old to be put to bed, but that night Anne sat with her. When Laney had first arrived, she'd slept in her own bed, but in a corner of Anne's large bedroom. When she turned nine, Anne and Norma built walls and a closet in Laney's bed area, leaving plenty of room for her large stuffed animal collection. This year Laney stored the animals under her bed and asked Anne to hang a full-length mirror on the closet door.

She felt feverish to Anne's touch and was talking the way she used to when she'd had too much chocolate. Anne calmed her with plans for the next day, helping Aunt Norma give Bark a bath and buying back-to-school supplies. She hoped Laney's impassioned sales pitch for a new cell-phone cover demonstrated a lack of interest in her mother's proposal to reclaim her.

The study smelled slightly of mold, reminding Anne that central air was a must as soon as she could afford it. She'd come into the room to keep her mind off the new development by finishing her bill paying. She compared the height of the unpaid to the paid stack of bills and felt defeated. Anyway, what she needed right now was someone to splash ice water in her face, give her some perspective. She needed to talk to Norma.

"…Norma Bergen here. Please be advised that I rarely listen to voicemail." Beep.

"Damn." When, an hour later, Anne was again put into Norma's voicemail, she considered dashing across the way to make sure her friend was all right. But what if Laney woke up while she was gone? She decided not to go. When had Norma ever needed help anyway?

7

Norma returned to her cottage to find Barclay "Bark" Bergen staring at the kitchen cabinet where his food was stored.

"Okay I'm late, but do you think after all these years you could get your own dinner?"

She shook the bag of dry dog food. Almost empty. "Don't give me the silent treatment. Passive aggressive goes both ways." She scratched his head and shook out the last sandy bits from the bottom of the bag.

With Bark settled, she gathered an armload of documents from her basement file cabinet and sat down at her desk in the converted dining room. The sun was beginning to set. She amused herself by giving the blazing scene a title, as though it were a painting hanging in a museum: *Radioactive Yolk, Punctured and Oozing.*

From her pile she extracted a thick manila folder and spread its contents across her desk. She ran her hand along the desk's uneven surface, reclaimed wood from an old ship, not from a town on the Cape but from Honfleur, a French seaport on the English Channel. She'd bought it from a Frenchman, Paul LaGarde. "Pole," as he pronounced his name, became her lover. She'd returned home six weeks later. As she later told Anne, she'd kept the wood, not the pole.

The label on the file read "Inn at Cockle Cove." She reached for her bag and pulled out the Summons and Complaint she'd received earlier and reread the Complaint, this time, carefully. The $10 million figure made her laugh. Even if the Temple brothers prevailed on all counts, they'd never collect that kind of money. But that was beside the point. She'd be broke before they even got through the discovery phase of litigation. The time she'd spend producing correspondence and memoranda wouldn't be so bad, but the electronic production would take serious time, first to gather the information and then to review it. There'd be the inevitable court battles over what was relevant, privileged, overbroad, and all the other bases for withholding information from the other side. She'd have no time for her own practice and no income. Being a sole practitioner had significant disadvantages at times like this.

She flipped to the document attached to the Complaint. It was a lengthy agreement between Mrs. Temple and her sons, signed by all the necessary parties and notarized. With growing anxiety she turned the pages until she reached paragraph twenty-one, a provision containing the right of first refusal language. "Where the hell'd that come from?" She reread the paragraph four times, each time hoping it would read differently. Throughout the process she repeated to herself, "Don't panic. You mustn't panic. Read it again."

The cover letter enclosed with the Complaint was signed by the Temple brothers' attorney. "Wouldn't you know, Derek Dohnan, a fuster cluck of the first order." She folded the letter into an airplane and sailed it across the room. "Isn't there some court rule prohibiting disgusting lawyers from practicing law?"

She retrieved the airplane and on her way back changed course and headed to the kitchen for a beer. The house was stuffy and hot and the blast of cold air from the open refrigerator provided relief. She opened the freezer door and stuck her face in, closing her eyes and thinking back to her first and only in-person encounter with Derek Dohnan.

At that time he was representing one of her clients in an employment discrimination case. They'd seen each other before at bar functions but had never spoken. He asked to meet her at The Lucky Duck for a quick lunch to discuss some aspects of his case.

As usual, the place was packed and they'd opted to sit at the bar rather than wait for a table. Seating at the bar was arranged so that customers could eat and drink and watch the crowds pass by on a quaint New England main street. Above the bar hung an old oil painting of drunken sailors and maidens in bacchanalian excess. Norma sat thigh by thigh with the loquacious Dohnan. He told her story after story, and every time he told what she knew was a lie, he pulled on an imaginary goatee, as if trying to redirect his receding chin.

She wanted desperately for him to stop talking and was on the verge of demanding it when a pudgy hand landed in her lap. At first she thought the windbag lawyer had mistakenly overshot his own leg, but then she remembered her cardinal rule—never give a lawyer the benefit of the doubt. She smiled at him, lifted his hairy mitt and shoved it into his own lap, causing his drink to splash all over his face and shirt. Contact thereafter was by email.

At the time she'd wondered why she'd been so upset about the incident and had come to realize it wasn't the vulgarity, but the inhumanity of his gesture. It was as though, over forty and single, she must welcome any male attention she could get and if she didn't, well, her wishes were irrelevant. The thought that he was now coming after her in a lawsuit got her adrenaline pumping. She said out loud, "Who was it who famously said, 'A little prick keeps a girl sharp'? Oh yes, *I* did."

Back at her desk, she tried to focus on the facts stated in the Complaint, picking out errors and making notes where follow-up was needed, but her mind kept straying to Laney's discovery of the dead man on the beach. She'd give anything if someone other than Lieutenant Coigne were investigating. Laney meant a lot to her. She didn't want the girl to feel vulnerable because of shady, shoddy police work, which is what she expected from a cop rumored to be dirty. The scene in Anne's living room came back to her and she realized with a jolt that Laney had been trying to ask her something, but she'd been too preoccupied getting rid of Coigne to listen. Maybe Laney had talked with Anne about whatever it was, but Norma knew there were some things Laney preferred to tell her rather than her grandmother. She'd have to find time tomorrow to talk to her in private.

A second beer eased her into a review of her due diligence subfile where all the transaction background documents were kept. She was horrified to find that her memory had played tricks on her. Contained in her file was the same agreement attached to the Complaint. "Oh hell!" She shuffled forward to paragraph twenty-one and found to her astonishment an integration clause, a boilerplate acknowledgement that the agreement was the complete and final accord between the parties. What she did not find in the agreement was a right of first refusal, even after a page-by-page, word-by-word review of her document. *What were Dohnan and the Temple brothers up to?*

Next she came to a "Memo to the File" that explained the purpose behind the sale of Mary's interest in Red River Resort. Long before Norma was involved, Mary had purchased the Red River interest, amounting to a fifty-one percent ownership, at a time when the resort was on the brink of bankruptcy and selling cheap. Her plan had been to eventually buy the rest of it for a song and achieve economies of scale by operating both her Inn at Cockle Cove and Red River Resort under one management. Later, when she needed cash to renovate the inn without incurring additional debt, she considered herself fortunate the other partners were willing to buy her out of the resort.

Norma put down the memo. "I don't get it." Her phone rang. She hated getting calls at night and wasn't going to answer, but relented. The caller spoke for some time. "Who is this?" When he spoke again she stood. "You should be talking to the police." She could barely hear him, which made her raise her own voice. "I can't meet you now."

At the caller's next word, Norma closed her eyes.

"Where do I meet you?"

8

From the moment she stuck her head in to wake Laney, Gran seemed distracted. Laney didn't know if it was because Gran was worried about her mom and Mr. Crawford or about Aunt Norma, an early riser who always stopped by for coffee but hadn't that morning. Gran had on her sleeveless purple blouse with the mandarin collar, which she always wore when she had something important to do.

"I can do that, Gran."

"I know, hon." She was picking up Laney's scattered clothes off the floor. "I just feel like doing it." Gran smiled at her with tired eyes. "What would you like to wear? How about the spaghetti-string sundress we bought in Boston? Sets off your golden locks."

Laney agreed with the choice, but would wait to dress until Gran left. She got up to make her bed. "Gran. How does Mom know Mr. Crawford? How would she know anyone here?"

Gran didn't answer and Laney wondered if she'd heard. Then she sat on the edge of the bed and patted the space next to her for Laney to sit down. "Your granddad and I used to come to the Cape all the time and bring your mother, starting when she was a baby. She loved to play in the woods and explore the marsh and the beach." Gran laughed. "She'd drag home anything she found—even a torpedo once. Good thing it was just the casing. After your granddad died, we came up here one last time." Gran turned away to smooth wrinkles in the bedspread.

"Why'd you stop coming?"

"Oh, well, your mother decided all of a sudden, it was just too bo-o-or-r-r-ring. It surprised me though. I always thought she was happy here, with her 'summer friends' as she called them. Maybe Mr. Crawford was a summer friend." She leaned over and kissed the top of Laney's head. "And then, before long, a beautiful baby was born and her name was...?"

"Me?"

"No, her name was Laney, silly. Anyway, you better hurry up. We need to be ready when your mom and Mr. Crawford arrive."

Laney found it hard to recognize her mother in her elegant green dress. The material was shantung, Gran called it. Her mother's pearl studs looked like little knots. She'd probably had red hair all along, but when had it ever looked so soft and wavy?

The ride to Red River Resort was quiet. She and Gran led the way in Gran's car, even though Laney would have preferred to ride with her mom in Mr. Crawford's Porsche. As they mounted the hotel steps to the veranda, Mr. Crawford whispered something to her mom, who shrugged, removed a wad of gum from her mouth and dropped it in a flower bed.

Gran leaned over and said in Laney's ear, "Now there goes the last trace of evidence this really is your mom." Laney smiled, even though she knew it wasn't quite nice. It reminded her of something Aunt Norma would say and she wished she had come with them.

The blast of air conditioning as the lobby doors opened made Laney glad Gran had insisted she bring a sweater. A whiff of sausage from the dining room reminded her how hungry she was. The maître d' greeted Mr. Crawford with a solemn nod, then led them into a vast dining room, sun-filled, with a panoramic view of the harbor and distant sail boats on Nantucket Sound.

There was drama everywhere, imposing white columns, fountains spurting blue water, and waiters dressed in black and white, rushing back and forth. The table settings dazzled with crystal glasses, polished silver, and thick white table cloths reaching all the way to the floor. Guests were seated by the windows for the view, but Laney's attention was drawn to the long buffet table in the center of the room. Her eyes widened at the ice sculpture shaped like a whale, surrounded by mounds of strawberries and pineapple. There were hunks of cheeses, frosted pastries, and copper hoods raised to present eggs, bacon, sausage, and pancakes. The array almost made her forget the purpose of the "breakfast meeting to set a course for Laney," as Mr. Crawford had called it.

"Sit next to Kenny, honey. May as well get used to him. He's going to be your dad."

"That's premature, Gin."

"Not so very, Mother." Gin wiggled her ring finger at Gran, which now had a large twinkling stone on it.

Laney's spirits sank as she thought of Mr. Crawford as her dad. He didn't fit her image of a father. She imagined someone who would cheer her up when she was sad by cracking jokes so dumb she'd have to laugh. And he'd help her become more athletic. Mr. Crawford looked like a celebrity and he wore cologne. He probably didn't know any dumb jokes and she didn't think he'd welcome a sweaty hug after practicing push-ups and pull-ups with her. *Why couldn't Mom just move in with Gran?*

The several forks and spoons by her plate confused Laney. She watched Gran for guidance, but Gran only shifted her knife back and forth as Mr. Crawford went on about property taxes.

Her mom's eyes roamed the room and when they reached the windows she blurted, "Look, Kenny, out there." She grabbed Mr. Crawford's chin and turned it. "A schooner. We need one of those. Wouldn't I look sexy in a bikini on that deck?"

Mr. Crawford didn't answer. His attention was caught by someone at the dining room entrance. Laney followed his gaze. Her heart thumped. Sandal Man stood next to the maître d'.

"Anne. May I call you Anne?" Mr. Crawford smiled at Gran. "We want to say how much we appreciate your watching after Laney while Gin was ill."

"Watching after?" Gran's tone was sharp, her face puckered up with new wrinkles. "I wasn't babysitting for an evening, Mr. Crawford. I've been raising my granddaughter for almost five years now."

Her eye on the dining room entrance, Laney sank low in her chair.

"Everyone knows you're a hero, Mother, saved the day and all that. But that's old news. Just look at me. Look at us." She placed her left hand over Mr. Crawford's.

Laney continued to sink.

The waiter arrived and explained how the buffet worked. He may have interrupted their argument, but not their angry thoughts, or they would have noticed Laney slipping beneath the table when they left for the buffet.

The waiter was refilling water glasses when they returned. Gran said, "My granddaughter must have gone to the ladies' room. She'll have orange juice please. Oh, pardon me."

Laney could tell someone had approached the table.

"You're looking well, Ken. And who are your lovely breakfast companions?"

Sandal Man. She recognized his voice. Had he seen her? Is that why he was here? She tried to hear their conversation but her panic shut down her senses.

At last she heard Mr. Crawford speak and realized Sandal Man and her Gran had left the table.

"When your mother gets back, let me handle her, Gin. And by the way, you should have gotten up, not your mother, to look for Laney in the ladies' room. Optics, Gin, optics. We talked about that."

Laney would try to remember to look up "optics," but her immediate problem was how to resurface without drawing attention, especially Sandal Man's. He could be seated anywhere. She was pretty certain there weren't any empty tables by the windows when he'd arrived. If she could just remain facing the windows with her back to the room. She rose quickly and grabbed her napkin from her seat as she sat down.

"What the hell?" Her mom was startled and almost tipped over her juice.

"I dropped my napkin and couldn't find it." Laney held it up as proof.

"Like hell you did." Her mom started to get mad, then laughed. "Can't say I blame you. I used to hide from Gran, too." Her mom winked at her, then looked at Mr. Crawford. He nodded.

"I've been looking everywhere for you." Gran returned to the table and scolded Laney for making her search, but her heart wasn't in it. When the waiter brought her orange juice and asked Laney if she was ready for the buffet, she whispered to Gran she had a stomach-ache and wasn't hungry. She didn't dare go to the buffet table and make herself visible to the room. To Laney's surprise, Gran let her stay seated, drink the juice, and eat the bread and rolls by her plate.

"What Gin is trying to say, Anne—"

"Let me get this straight, Mr. Crawford. You're trying to translate for *me* what *my* daughter is saying. I really think...."

Laney never heard what Gran thought. Her eyes locked on Sandal Man. She closed them instantly, but not before seeing surprise and recognition in his.

"What do you have to say about it, baby? You want to live with Kenny and me, don't you?"

Laney couldn't bear it another moment: her mother's sugary voice, Gran's outrage, the smell of Mr. Crawford's cologne, and most of all, her fear of Sandal Man. Tears rolled down her cheeks. "I want to go home."

"You see!" Her mom thrust her arm across the table as if to say, "Voila!"

Gran pushed back her chair. "That's not what she means. Come on, Laney. Let's get you *home*."

Inside the car, Laney's silent tears turned into loud sobbing. Gran held her, saying, "You don't have to go anywhere, you're staying with me," until the sobbing wound down to an occasional shudder. The only sounds on the drive home were Laney's hiccups and the faint strains of classical music on the radio. At last the burden of holding onto her secret was too heavy. Laney opened her mouth to speak, but Gran cut her off.

"I want to do the right thing by you, Laney. If I thought your mom was able to take care of you, I would let you go."

Even with her other worries, Laney wondered if Gran meant what she said. What did it matter? She didn't know what she wanted, other than not to be so afraid.

9

"You okay back there?"

Norma made a croaking sound, somewhere between a groan of pain and a warning for Coigne to mind his own business. She cradled her right arm, which had been twisted so far up her back she was amazed it hadn't dislocated. A glance in the cruiser's side mirror showed her a bloodied nose so frightening she closed her swollen eyes.

Coigne started the cruiser. "You going to tell me what happened? And don't say you just fell down."

"Of course I won't tell you I fell down. I'm not one of your domestic abuse victims."

"I wouldn't say you were anyone's victim."

Coigne sounded like he admired her. She wasn't sure why. She'd done everything she could to annoy him.

"Just give me the headlines, Norma. We'll get the details when you're feeling better."

"Fine. I got a call around 9:00 last night. Guy said he had important information for me. I met him right where you found me, and as you can see, that was a mistake."

Coigne had stumbled on her that morning, as he was out early at the crime scene and getting a feel for the neighborhood. He'd tried to call an ambulance for her.

"Don't get carried away, Coigne," she'd said. "Just drive me home. I've got a dog to let out."

They compromised on a trip to the Urgicenter for an x-ray. He'd eased her into the back seat and strapped her in a seat belt.

Coigne sped down Route 28 and turned onto an unnamed road leading to the Urgicenter. Everyone thought it odd that a town would overlook naming the road where emergency medical services were provided. Norma's explanation was that, like everything else on the Cape, conservation was behind it. What was being conserved was emergency medical services.

"You know who it was who called you? You recognize the voice?"

"Nope."

They pulled into the parking lot. It was crowded for 8:00 a.m., but not for Fourth of July weekend. Norma tried to open her door with her left arm reaching across her body but had trouble.

"Sit still. I'll get it."

They made it to the entrance and Coigne held open the door. "It just doesn't sound like you, Norma, going out to meet a stranger at night. How did he get you to meet him?"

She knew what Coigne was up to. Officer Friendly was back and looking for information. He'd stick with her, opening doors and acting concerned, until he got what he wanted. T'was ever thus. She wasn't going to tell him the caller had used Laney's name to lure her to the meet. Instinctively she knew to keep Laney out of it. Still, if Coigne hadn't come along when he did, she'd still be stuck head first in a hydrangea bush. For all her bravado now, she'd been terrified last night. Her attacker had instructed her to meet him just a few blocks from home. He approached from behind. Without a sound, he whipped her around, punched her face three times, and tossed her away like a sack of dirty laundry. By the time her self-defense lessons clicked in, her nostrils were full of dirt. Next thing she knew, it was morning and Coigne was rolling her over. She guessed she owed Coigne something.

"I had the impression the caller had information about yesterday's drowning. That's why I met him."

"Why'd you think that?"

"Because he said so."

"Why didn't you call me?"

"He said not to call the police."

The wall-to-wall carpeting in the waiting room smelled new. People sat or leaned against the walls and to Norma, they all looked hung over.

Registration took forever, resulting in her barely making it to the ladies' room in time. There, she took care of business, blotted her face with a wet paper towel, and took a good look in the mirror. Her nose looked bad. She'd probably leave the Urgicenter with a white bandage pyramid in the middle of her face. She rejoined Coigne and he gave her a cup of coffee from the vending machine.

"Here. I brought some cream and sugar too."

Norma let him doctor her drink, but before she could take a sip they called her down the hall for an examination and x-ray. When she returned, the coffee was stone cold but she drank it anyway. An hour later she complained to a passing nurse, "How long does it take to read an x-ray? I've been here hours."

"The doctor will be with you soon."

"That's what you said before."

"You're welcome," she said, with a friendly wave as she kept moving.

The news was good, nothing broken. She came away with a few stitches, a sling, a prescription, and a throbbing headache. She wanted to sleep for a week.

Coigne's questions continued right up to her front door. It was unlocked, just as she'd left it, but something was wrong. "Bark?" She rushed in. "Where are you, boy? Bark? Barclay!"

Coigne followed her in and stopped dead. "Ho-ly shit!"

The cottage was torn apart—curtains yanked from the windows, books swept off shelves, files emptied onto the floor. In the kitchen, the refrigerator door was propped open by a vegetable bin pulled out of its track and juice from a broken pickle jar converged with spilled milk.

Norma was blind to the wanton destruction. She found Bark by the back door, lying on his side. Deep grooves on the doorframe showed how hard he'd tried to escape. Norma ran her hand down his flank, still warm, but *still*. She placed her finger in the hole in his head, the source of the red pool his black fur was soaking in. From far away she heard Coigne on his phone.

Norma hadn't cried since she was a girl. She wouldn't now.

Coigne called from the living room. "Got the crime scene guys coming. Forensics. You there, Norma?"

He found her lying beside Bark, humming softly in his ear.

"Oh no. I'm so sorry, Norma."

She sat up. "You should be. If we'd come here first like I wanted to he might still be alive."

Coigne paused, then left her alone and only returned when she opened the back door. He explained that she couldn't move the dog or bury him until the bullet was removed. He got on his phone again, supplementing his earlier report with details about Bark.

Norma walked to the edge of her yard. Down the bluff the tide was receding. She thought of all the years she and Bark had walked to the beach at the beginning and end of each day for their silent, companionable stroll, as necessary to one as the other. The pounding surf made her think of the dead man who'd rolled in with it just yesterday. He and Bark had died for the same reason. They were impediments to someone's plans.

"Norma?" Coigne had followed her outside.

She didn't answer. She was too busy connecting dots. The intruder was a killer, of her dog, certainly, and maybe of the dead man. That killer knew Laney's name.

10

Norma burst through Anne's front door and interrupted a Scriabin piece, among Anne's favorites. "Where's Laney? I've got to see her. Now!"

"God, Norma. What's happened to you? Your face. Your arm."

Even though Norma had changed into a clean white T-shirt and tan drawstring pants, she still looked like she'd been in the ring. "I'll fill you in later. Where's Laney?" Without waiting for an answer she lunged toward the stairwell. "Laney?"

"No, Norma. She's outside. I think she went out to find Bark for his bath. She's probably looking for you. What's going on?"

At the mention of her dog, Norma clenched the banister.

"Hey. Norma."

"I'm sorry, Anne. I must sound like a nut. I had a bad night, as you can see, and ought to be lying down. I've got this bee in my bonnet about that man Laney found yesterday and want to ask her a few questions, that's all. I promise I'll explain everything when I get back."

Only by extracting further assurances that Norma was all right and would return soon to explain, would Anne let her go.

Cutting behind the house, Norma sprinted toward the beach. Her arm hurt like hell.

"This sling is crap." She flung it away.

Signs at the entrance to the beach directed dog walkers to use the beach path that paralleled the shore. She figured if Laney had gone to her house when she and Coigne were out back, she'd next try the dog path.

The sun was in her eyes, but shielding them with her good hand, she thought she made out a pink top and white shorts heading west.

"Laney!"

The wind carried her voice and the figure turned. As they drew closer, Norma could see the girl had been crying.

Laney grew limp in Norma's arms as the gruff woman hugged her and patted her back. "Your Gran didn't tell me you were upset."

"I told her I was looking for Bark, but I was really looking for you. I need to tell somebody something, but I'm—what happened to you?"

"Forget about that. You're what?"

Laney didn't answer.

"Let's go find a bench to sit on," Norma said. "We can talk better if we're watching sailboats."

They left the path and mounted a steep hill to an overlook nicknamed Makeout Point. Norma bit her lip with each step and wondered whether she should have kept the sling. They emerged into a clearing and, to Norma's relief, found an empty bench.

"Did Gran tell you about Mom and Mr. Crawford?"

"I didn't give her a chance to tell me anything."

Laney explained about her mom's surprise visit, the marriage plans and the arguments at breakfast. Norma didn't cross-examine, nor did she express her disapproval at the prospect of Laney's living with her mom. Only when Laney finished her story did she start to probe.

"The man with your mom, you called him Mr. Crawford. Is that Kenneth Crawford, the big shot who owns Red River Resort?" She thumbed in the direction of the resort cottages and facilities sprawled along the beachfront.

"I think so. Mom called him Ken."

"Hm."

They watched a windsurfer sweep by.

"Do you know him, Aunt Norma?"

"I might."

Norma wondered how the hell Gin Sager, Little Miss Debauchery, knew Ken Crawford. But maybe the twosome wasn't that improbable. Back when she represented the Inn at Cockle Cove, Norma had heard of Ken Crawford. He'd been among the resort partners when Mary Temple sold her resort interest. There were rumors about him, that maybe he'd bullied his partners in some way. Nothing was ever proved, or at least nothing stuck, not because he was an honest person, they said, but because he was slick. She'd heard he was now one of just two partners who owned the resort.

Guys like Crawford would always be successful because they were clever, without qualm, and full of charm. It was the charm part that fascinated Norma. Having none of her own, she never succumbed to it in others. This immunity prevented her from understanding how others fell prey to it.   But what in the world would a guy like Crawford see in Gin? Fixed up, Gin might be attractive, but men like Crawford were not vulnerable in that way. Besides, while Crawford might use arm candy for his own purposes, last time Norma saw Gin, she looked more like tooth decay.

There was a mystery here and the fact that it involved Laney aroused Norma's protective instincts. She'd need to explore a tender subject like Laney's mother with great care.

"What's eating you, Laney? I should have thought you'd be pretty happy having your mom show up with plans to stay around."

"I am. It's just that I wish Gran and Mom could make up and live together, with me, at Gran's house."

Norma noted the omission of Mr. Crawford from the rosy fantasy.

"I'm not going to sugarcoat it for you, kid. I don't see that happening. Your mom and Gran are too different. There's so much history there, disappointment and misunderstanding, going both ways, I'd imagine."

Laney gathered a wad of her hair into the side of her mouth. They both watched a gull glide overhead, a clam in its talons. It hovered over the nearby parking lot and dropped the clam. The maneuver failed to open the shell. The gull swooped in again, snapped up its payload, soared high and released. This time it worked.

The show over, Laney went on with her story. "There's something else, something I forgot to tell everybody about the drowning. There was this man." She stopped talking to rearrange the wad of hair in her mouth.

Norma wondered if this new habit would replace or coexist with the blinking. It was all she could do to keep from yanking the wad out of her mouth. "Go on."

Laney told her about Sandal Man, including his showing up at the resort dining room.

Norma was on the verge of yelling, "You didn't think to mention this? You could have been talking to the murderer!" But then she remembered, Laney had tried to tell her something when she was busy getting rid of Coigne yesterday and she suspected it was about Sandal Man. "Have you told your Gran yet?"

"I was going to, but she seems so upset about my mom and Mr. Crawford, I just can't find the right time."

Norma knew she was in no position to scold Laney for withholding important information. She too was holding onto facts relevant to Coigne's investigation. The man who called her last night tied Laney's name to the drowning. The caller may have been Sandal Man, except he didn't have a foreign accent. Still, something about Laney's description of Sandal Man struck her as familiar.

"Things are going to work out, Laney. We'll talk to Gran and Lieutenant Coigne. He's probably got Sandal Man in custody right now. What do you want to bet?"

11

Anne pressed her hand to her heart. She felt as if she were having a heart attack. Visits by her daughter tended to cause this sensation. All those years, Gordon had served as buffer between them. Now, she had to coach herself before an encounter with Gin just to maintain her calm. It was all too much: Gin's sudden appearance with plans to marry Ken Crawford and reclaim Laney, a murder at their back door, the horrifying home invasion at Norma's and to top it off, she'd just offended Norma.

Laney and Norma had returned from the beach and Laney retreated to her drums in the garage. Anne had hoped her granddaughter would play the piano, experiencing the same joy she'd felt the first time she'd recognized a ghost-like melody hiding in the base, or when she'd finally developed her technique so that the keys could sound like a river when played just so. But one day her granddaughter arrived home from school with a block of wood, drum sticks, and a surprising sense of rhythm. She still would have pushed Laney to give piano a chance except Norma convinced her not to. She said Laney found solace in pounding out a beat at ever-increasing tempos and to let her be. Anne consoled herself with the knowledge that at least drums, like the piano, were percussion instruments.

Norma joined Anne in the kitchen. They peeled potatoes at the sink while Norma filled her in on how she'd been injured and the trashing of her home. Anne stopped peeling when Norma told her of Bark's death. She held her friend close until Norma said, "I'm okay. Let's peel."

"What the hell was this guy after, Norma?"

"Beats me."

Norma's quick answer made Anne wonder if she knew more than she was telling and it turns out, she did. After a long pause, Norma put down her potato. "The caller used Laney's name. That's how he convinced me to meet him. He knew she'd discovered the body."

Anne threw down her potato. "How? How could he know?"

"I don't know, exactly, but there's more." Norma told her about Sandal Man.

"Why did she tell *you* all this?"

"Is that really important now? The priority is to contact Coigne and fill him in."

"Why didn't you insist that we take Laney to his office yesterday? You should have known better. You're the lawyer."

Norma seemed paralyzed at first. Then she gathered her potato skins and dropped them into the trash.

"Norma, I shouldn't have said that. I'm sorry."

"You know, criticizing my legal skills for a bad result is a bit like my criticizing your parenting skills. Do you want to go there or should we take Laney to see Coigne now?"

On the way to the Barracks, Norma contacted Coigne and gave him a vague outline of what they wanted to tell him. She also filled Anne and Laney in on how investigations work on the Cape, with the district attorney, or DA, assigning state troopers, like Lieutenant Coigne, to get to the bottom of things. She said sometimes the state troopers work with local police and anyone else who can help solve the crime. The tutorial over, everyone pursued their own thoughts and the drive seemed to take forever. The steady hum of Norma's balding tires took the place of conversation.

Coigne met them at the entrance. "Norma. Ms. Sager." He smiled at Laney. "Let's go to my office." He led them down a narrow, carpeted hallway. "How are you feeling now, Norma?"

"Dandy."

Anne said, "Have you been able to identify the murder victim?"

"Let's wait until we sit down, Ms. Sager."

They arrived at a glass-paneled door. Coigne stepped aside to let Anne and Laney go in first. Norma made a scooting motion for him to precede her.

"Just so you know," Norma said, "we're here for an informal meeting to discuss some additional information that has only just come to light."

"Understood."

"So, Lieutenant Coigne, who was he?" Anne asked.

Coigne centered himself to face Anne. "Guy named Bradford Todd."

She almost gasped. *Did I hear him correctly?* She struggled to hide her shock.

"They called him Buddy. A local guy, his family owned a lot of property for years, but they sold it, they died off, and he became a low-life drifter."

Norma took over the questioning. "How old?"

"Thirty-two."

"Interesting. Who identified him?"

"Skaket Seaside Inn contacted us. Said a guest had been with them for several months, then left without paying up and taking his things. Hotel clerk made a positive ID. Said Buddy Todd had talked with him about a meeting with a lawyer. Todd was super mad about something, according to the guy."

"Who was the lawyer?"

"Dohnan? Know him?

"If it's Derek Dohnan, I know him. He's with Pissin', Moanin', Dunscombe and Dohnan."

Coigne's eyebrows shot up.

"Dunscombe and Dohnan. I made up the other names as a mnemonic—they fit so well. What else did you learn?"

Coigne hid a smile as he spoke about the steps his office had taken in the investigation, but gave little away about where those steps had led. Anne used the time to pull herself together. She'd have to tell Coigne and Norma how she knew Buddy Todd, but not with Laney in the room. She stole a look at her granddaughter, who was, thank God, showing no signs of anxiety.

Anne perused the spartan office. The only personal item was a photograph on the desk of a short man, probably in his sixties, wearing a police uniform. He had his arm around a boy who was squinting, probably facing the sun. She wondered if the boy was Coigne and if the man was his grandfather.

Coigne offered them coffee and soda. The accommodation and Coigne's general courtesy surprised her, as their encounter in her living room the day before had been unpleasant. They accepted his peace offerings and Laney slipped out to the ladies' room.

"Before you question Laney, I need to tell you something I forgot to mention." Norma said that her caller the night before had mentioned Laney by name as the person who discovered the body.

"Forgot to mention? This pretty much confirms the break-in and assault on you was tied to the drowning. You should have said something sooner, Norma."

Norma raised her hands in surrender. "I'm guilty of a bad memory. Shoot me."

When Laney returned, Coigne softened his voice. "I understand you met a man on the beach, Laney. You call him Sandal Man. Tell us everything you can remember about the encounter. Let's start with what he looked like."

Coigne wasn't taking notes and Anne hadn't seen a recording device. He was probably trying to help Laney relax, but she thought he'd regret not jotting down some of Laney's impressive detail.

So strange, the things young people remembered, things she never would have noticed. Laney said Sandal Man wore a watch with diamonds and a silver bracelet with a black stone. His sandals were well-worn but looked soft, with a circle brace for the big toe. She even described the man's tie, which had a small sheep wrapped in a blanket.

Coigne said, "A sheep? Odd thing on a tie. May be worth pursuing."

"You won't find a tie like it on the Cape," Anne said. "If I'm right, that sheep is the logo for Brooks Brothers. My father only wore—"

53

"Wait a minute," Norma said. "I knew there was something about Laney's description of Sandal Man that rang a bell. Almost ran into a guy dressed in business clothes yesterday afternoon. I called him 'Brooks Brothers.' I was too intent on getting my mail to give him much thought."

Norma gave a run-down of the time and where the man had appeared to be headed, but had no other details.

"Go ahead, Laney," Coigne said.

"We had breakfast at Red River Resort this morning. I think it was Sandal Man who came to our table but I didn't get a good look at him then. I recognized his voice. I saw him later and he looked the same as on the beach, except he wasn't wearing sandals."

Coigne turned to Anne. "You were with your granddaughter. You must have seen him, too."

"I barely looked at him. I was headed out of the dining room when he showed up." She thought back and tried to picture him. Laney's description of Sandal Man on the beach, dark skin, large brown eyes, and thin lips, could have been the man at the table. She couldn't say it out loud but most dark-skinned men in business suits looked alike to her. "My granddaughter is giving you a better description than I can. I will say this: The man who can identify him would be my daughter's fiancé, Ken Crawford. They spoke to each other, but Mr. Crawford didn't even introduce him. I don't think he wanted Sandal Man around."

"Ken Crawford?" Coigne pushed on his desk, rolling his chair backwards. "You're talking about the guy who owns Red River Resort?"

Anne could see he was disturbed. "What is it, Lieutenant?"

"Yes, what's the big deal about Crawford?" Norma asked.

Coigne didn't answer. Instead, he pulled open his desk drawer and reached inside. His look of intense concentration turned into a smile. When he withdrew his hand it held three lollipops. He doled them out. "A reward for coming in." He stood. "I am so sorry, ladies. I forgot the time. I'm afraid I've got to take another meeting. And Norma—give me a call later today.

Anne was furious. "Just like that? He dismisses us without anything more than a-a sucker? How belittling."

They were on their way back to Norma's car. Laney had already unwrapped her lollipop and gone to drop the wrapper in a trash can. Norma was struggling with her wrapper, which was sticking to the green candy. "Oh hell." She dropped it into her bag. "What did you expect, Anne?"

Anne had expected Coigne to praise them for coming forward. They were delivering a "person of interest" on a silver platter. "I'd hoped Coigne would get on the phone, then and there, get identification of the dark man from Ken Crawford and this ordeal would be over."

"It's not like a made for TV movie called, 'Beach Murder,' Anne. Think 'Masterpiece Theater.' The investigation may go on a long time."

"And why, as we were leaving, do you suppose Coigne asked you to give him a call? I didn't think you could tolerate each other."

"How should I know?"

Anne pondered for the rest of the way home and was able to figure out two things. First, Coigne just wanted to talk further when Laney wasn't around, about the possible tie-in between the drowned man and the assault on Norma the night before. That's why he asked Norma to call him later. Second, based on Norma's sulky, 'how-should-I-know?' response, she hadn't quite forgiven Anne the earlier attack on her legal skills, obviously a sensitive subject for her right now.

12

Anne sighed at the sight of Gin's car when they pulled into the driveway. She hoped Crawford wasn't inside with her daughter. If he were, she'd have to tell him to contact the police about his chum, Sandal Man. And what kind of man was Ken Crawford, having such a colleague, or friend, or whatever he was?

Norma said she'd be in touch. Normally she'd toot her horn good-bye, but this time she just backed out of the driveway. Still miffed.

Gin was standing alone in the center of the living room, wine glass in hand, wine bottle half-empty. "I guess you're happy now, Mother." She didn't appear to notice Laney. "You couldn't stand to see me happy, could you? You had to scare him away."

What a difference. Only this morning Gin had looked—yes, Anne had to admit she had looked beautiful. Now, her eyes were swollen, cheeks pale, and the coral lipstick that had gone so well with her hair color had been gnawed away. Her lip liner made a bull's eye around her tight mouth. "What do you mean, Gin, scared him away?" Anne tossed her purse on the couch. "I would have thought that was more in your line."

Gin gulped the rest of her drink and slammed it down.

Anne wished she hadn't said that. "I apologize, Gin. That was uncalled for. I'm saying all the wrong things today. Why don't I make us some coffee?"

"Don't bother, Mother." She poured herself another glass of wine.

"I'll make some anyway." Anne started to leave, then had second thoughts. "How about a snack, Laney? Come on."

"Stay here with me, baby."

"Oh for God's sake, Gin."

Laney obeyed neither one. She left the room and headed upstairs. The closing of her bedroom door made a quiet click.

"Still got the old touch, Mother."

Anne knew better than to respond. Every word, well-intended or not, would trigger prolonged combat. Gin's distress seemed real. Anne could see that. What wasn't clear was whether Gin really believed Anne was the cause of Ken's supposed disappearance. There was something more worried than angry about her accusation. It was as though Gin had only slipped back into her old whining, accusing ways because it was familiar and safe territory.

How in the world to deal with Gin. She wished her daughter would leave. Gordon had once asked her in his gentle way not to make Gin feel so inadequate. Anne had snapped, "Why shouldn't I? She is, you know." She'd never forget his look of shock.

"Tell me what's happened, Gin. I am listening. What makes you think he's gone?"

"I need some air." Gin strutted out to the deck, taking her glass and bottle with her. She left the door open and Anne took that to mean she was willing to talk if Anne would grovel a bit and follow her.

They stretched out on chaise lounges, a barrel of dahlias between them. Having followed her out, Anne felt it was now Gin's turn to make a move. She killed time studying the clouds, making out a floating medieval fortress heading east toward Europe. Someone across the marsh was grilling burgers and the aroma made her salivate.

"We were going to go look at that schooner. That one we saw this morning. He was going to . . ."

"What? Ken was going to what?"

"He was going to see if it was for sale. When he didn't show up, I called everywhere I could think of."

"Did you try his office?"

"Of course I tried his office. His secretary says no one knows where he is. That bitch is lying. I can hear it in her voice." Gin rolled away, turning her back to Anne.

Anne watched her shoulders shake and thought about giving her a hug. Or should she offer her hope by telling her Lieutenant Coigne was going to be contacting Crawford, so he'd surely show up soon? That wouldn't help Gin, though. Anne guessed she wasn't worried Crawford had actually vanished into thin air. She was worried he'd dumped her, an all-too-common occurrence in her unhappy life. But this time Gin may have been trying hard to keep him.

Gin rolled back over, wiping her cheeks with her hands. When had her daughter looked so desolate? Yes, it was that last summer they'd come to the Cape, after Gordon had died. Anne had tended to brush off her daughter's sad looks as teenage drama and based on her observations of the past hour, this might be more of the same. With Gin it was hard to tell whether she was experiencing true sorrow or was simply frustrated at not getting what she wanted. Anne reached over and patted her knee.

13

As they were walking back from Makeout Point earlier in the day, Aunt Norma had told Laney that Bark had died. Without Bark, Laney had no friend her own age, human or canine. She'd asked if he had been hit by a car. Aunt Norma only swallowed hard and looked away.

Laney examined the photo on top of her dresser. It was taken during a sleepover at Aunt Norma's when she and Bark had curled up together after a long day at the beach. She hugged the framed photo, kissed her finger, and pressed it against the glass.

Head on pillow, eyes closed, Laney tried to lose herself in the drum solo pounding through her earbuds. If only school would start. Not that she was a fan of homework, but anything that plucked her from the war room downstairs had to be an improvement. What if one of the kids from school was passing by her house and overheard her drunken mother yelling at Gran?

It wasn't that she harbored hopes of joining Isabella Miller's crowd. Just one good friend would do. At school she worked on appearing indifferent, throwing herself into music, ignoring the kids who hung out together between classes. She suspected they all knew she was a lonely loser anyway.

Aunt Norma usually helped her solve her problems, or at least shrink them. Laney had hoped she would make Sandal Man disappear and send Ken Crawford packing in the bargain. Unlike Gran, who sometimes didn't get what the problem was, Aunt Norma understood right away and could explain things so they weren't so scary anymore. This time, confiding in Aunt

Norma only made things worse. That place they'd dragged her to! She could just picture it. While the other kids talked about soccer camp in Italy and hiking down the Grand Canyon, she'd have to say the highlight of her summer was spent in the State Police Barracks.

Laney swung her body around to her favorite position, head lolling over the bedside and legs propped straight up against the wall. She wished Gran wouldn't check on her at night and shift her head back onto her pillow. She wasn't a baby.

Maybe she should run away. The last time she'd tried she'd been about five years old. Her underpants with the red ruffles and her mom's sunglasses were essentials that had fit nicely into an old patent leather cosmetics bag. She hadn't been running away exactly, just heading to Gran's. It amazed her still that she had complete confidence she would find her way on foot from Philadelphia to Cape Cod. It was only when the police brought her to the station and they couldn't reach her mom that she cried.

The flashback to the police reminded her of something Lieutenant Coigne had said. Gran had just asked about the name of the beach murder victim, Buddy Todd. She'd heard the name before and remembered it because it seemed funny for someone to have a name like Buddy, and a first name, Todd, for a last name. *What did all that have to do with running away?*

Her unsuccessful flight from home long ago discouraged her from running away now. At least a bike ride into town would get her away from the household drama and who knew, maybe she'd see someone from school. A couple of times when she'd come upon a classmate who was alone, they'd hung out together. Laney brightened at the prospect and changed into a light blue T-shirt emblazoned with a shark, like Isabella wore. She chose pale blue glass earrings to match her shirt and a braided anklet to hide the scar on her ankle, which Aunt Norma said no one but the freckle next to it could see. After scrutinizing herself in the mirror she removed a clip from her hair, bent over, and quickly flipped her head back. Her long blond hair fell in a wave across her forehead, covering the zit she'd discovered that morning. "Not great, better."

The new bike path, from Skaket to Potonumecot, was only a two-minute bike ride from home. She heard Gran and her mom out on the deck and decided to leave them alone. Her mom sounded unhappy. Gran would want to know where Laney was headed and might say she couldn't go.

She rolled her bike out of the cool garage and stepped into heavy humidity. A fleeting image of Sandal Man, when he'd spotted her in the resort dining room, made her hesitate. "Nuts to that." She fastened her helmet.

14

"Iyannough! That Indian may have gotten off easy. Died young. Come to think of it, a lot of Indians who helped the Pilgrims died young."

Norma was talking to herself in bumper-to-bumper traffic on her way to the Law Offices of Dunscombe and Dohnan. Even before they'd left Coigne's office, she'd decided to drop off Anne and Laney, turn around, and get right back on the road. Traffic on Chief Iyannough's eponymous road was murder during tourist season, especially afternoon rush hour. Her sour mood turned fetid in the suffocating humidity as her air conditioning didn't work.

She'd once told Anne the story of how her father made the family ride around all summer with the car windows closed tight so neighbors would think they had air conditioning. This was before air conditioning was standard equipment.

"That must have been pure torture, Norma."

"Yep."

"It explains why you never waste your time trying to keep up with the Joneses."

"You mean I don't put on 'airs'?"

"Very funny."

Norma didn't think Anne was right. She believed she was quite capable of exhibiting all character failings, including envy, but her short fuse was so powerful and ever present, it made her other flaws barely noticeable.

Her mind shifted to events of the night before. The wild destruction of her home led her to believe the intruder hadn't found what he was after, or at least not early in his search. But what worried her more was the gratuitous nature of the physical harm, the punches in the face, the slaughter of her poor dog. Those things weren't necessary and added to the risk the guy would get caught. Was there someone out there who hated her that much? No. The man who hit her was detached and professional, not emotional. So how did that narrow the field?

She thought about Coigne, his attention to her injuries, and seemingly genuine compassion over Bark's death. "Goddammit. Does this mean I'm going to have ambivalent feelings about a dirty cop?" Norma prided herself on the accuracy of her first impressions. "Absolutely not."

Her cell phone rang and she rummaged in her bag for it.

"—lo."

"Coigne here. Got a minute?"

"Shoot."

"Sounds like you're in the car. Call me back after you've pulled over."

"I've got Bluetooth." That was a lie. So much for not putting on airs.

"First of all, how are you feeling?"

"Hold on while I hum a few bars of 'You'll Never Walk Alone.' What's on your mind, Coigne?"

"No small talk, then. Ken Crawford is dead. Hit and run on a dirt road. From all we can determine, the last one to see him alive was Gin Sager."

"Whoa! Where was the accident?"

"Probably not an accident. Looks like he was run over several times. We'll know for sure once we take a look at photos, the glass and paint analysis, and the medical examiner's report. Shouldn't be hard to tell, though. They say the tire treads are clear as handprints at Grauman's Chinese."

"I get it. So where?"

"Side road off Pilgrim Road in Cockle Cove."

Traffic slowed to a full stop. "You knew all this when Anne and I brought Laney to the Barracks. You cut the meeting short when Anne said Ken Crawford's name. Why wait until now to say anything about it?"

"Wouldn't you agree the murder of one father is enough for any thirteen-year-old to handle?"

"That's an odd way to put it, but I guess you're right. Crawford was Gin's fiancé and that would make him Laney's future stepfather." Traffic started moving. "What do you mean, 'one father is enough'?"

"You tell me."

What the hell? Norma waited him out.

"Don't you think Laney can be better protected if you start playing straight with me, Norma?"

"I assure you I am."

"Christ. You don't think the fact the dead guy on the beach was Laney's father is relevant?"

"What? Buddy Todd? Nonsense. Where'd you get that?"

"Are you asking me to believe you didn't know he was her biological father?"

"I'm not asking you to believe anything, gum wad. I don't think Laney's own mother knows who the father is, so how would I know?"

No one spoke, then, "Let's step back, Norma. Did Laney act like she recognized the drowned man when she first broke the news of her discovery?"

It was ridiculous, but Norma played along. She pictured Laney as she'd stood at the front door the day before, pale, freckles larger than acorns, and shocked, like anyone would be. "No way. She did not know him. Anyway, how do *you* know the guy's her father?"

"Hard to argue with DNA. Found the report in his room. Gin applied for child support a long time ago and Buddy Todd had the lab test results. He also had baby photos of Laney with her mother, at least it looks like Gin Sager from a mug shot we have. It was all there in his hotel room, like it was waiting to be found. Beyond all that, Anne Sager confirmed it by phone. There's more follow-up we need to do, but the evidence looks good."

Norma was staggered by the news about Buddy Todd's relationship to Laney and just as shocked that Anne had said nothing to her about Laney's father before. She pulled into the law firm's parking lot and turned off her ignition. "Go on."

"I'm seeing obvious connections—Laney sees Sandal Man, then discovers a dead body who turns out to be her own father, then Sandal Man runs into Laney's future stepfather at Red River Resort, now future step-father's dead, likely murdered. I don't think these are coincidences. Whether she knows why or not, Laney Sager is somehow in the middle of all this."

"It doesn't necessarily follow, Coigne. Laney didn't know her father and barely knew Ken Crawford. Her mother knew both of them. What does she have to say?"

"The man who called you last night mentioned Laney's name, not Gin's, and tied Laney's name to the body on the beach. That doesn't prove these murders have any more to do with Laney than her mother or anyone else, but there are enough ties to Laney for me to be concerned for her safety. *And* her mother's."

"Then get off the phone and find Sandal Man."

15

Norma stayed in her car and parsed through Coigne's revelations and conclusions. He was right about one thing. Until they had this Sandal Man in custody, they needed to keep an eye on Laney. She phoned Anne.

"It's me. I'm in a hurry now, but I need to talk to you and Laney when I get back. Can you two stay put? It's important, Anne."

"No problem. She's upstairs. We'll be here."

Confident that Laney was safe, Norma focused on her other problem, the lawsuit. Something smelled rotten about the suit and if she could pinpoint the source, and satisfy herself she could get the suit dismissed quickly, her mind would clear and she'd be in a better position to help in the murder investigation.

The law firm of Dunscombe and Dohnan was in a strip mall wedged between Danang Nails and School of Tai Chi. Norma was surprised to find the firm's reception area well-appointed with slate-colored furnishings, sconces that gave off an attractive ambient glow, and one or two good paintings. It was nothing like her grand firm in Boston that had impressed her in her early days. She'd learned to appreciate paintings by protégées of Mary Cassatt and John Singer Sargent, not on the walls of the Museum of Fine Arts, but down the pearl grey hallways of her law firm. By contrast, a good law firm on the Cape mounted paint-by-number seascapes. Still, the not-too-distant view of Nantucket Sound from Dunscombe and Dohnan's plate glass window outclassed anything her old firm had to offer.

The office was quiet, no waiting clients, no sounds of Dohnan blustering in the conference room, just the click-click of meteoric typing.

"Can I help you?" The receptionist, a slim man in his mid-twenties, stubble beard, elbows tucked in, barely lifted one of his furious fingers to point toward a chair.

"Is Mr. Dohnan or Mr. Dunscombe in?"

"Both at depos. They'll be back in"—he glanced at his watch—"one hour and thirty-seven minutes. Can I *help* you?"

Norma had rehearsed several approaches for getting information out of Dohnan. Instead, she'd have to work on his guard dog. "I'm one of the lawyers involved in the Cockle Cove-Temple litigation. I'd like to check on some facts in the files." She wasn't lying. She was "involved" in the litigation and she definitely wanted to get into the files.

"Like I say, they'll be back in—one hour and thirty-six minutes."

The receptionist pushed the print button and Norma had to raise her voice to be heard over the machine. "Too bad." She checked *her* watch. "I don't think they'll like missing a 5:00 deadline."

"What deadline?"

"That's just how it always goes. No one ever gives you the information you need to do your job. And then they'll take it out on you." Norma started to leave, saying just loud enough to be heard, "It would take until 5:00 to even find the file, no doubt."

"Wanna bet? Name the file and follow me."

Norma had correctly detected strong organization skills in the receptionist and guessed he took tremendous pride in them.

She followed his squared shoulders down the hall to a file room, then onward to the door marked Derek Dohnan, Esq. He placed three accordion files on Dohnan's desk.

"These are the most recent files," he said.

"And if I need to look at other files, should I go back to the file room?"

"Or just call me. I'll find them."

"*Or* just call me," Norma said to herself. "That means I can go myself or call him. I'll go myself."

Her plan was to nose around in Dohnan's Cockle Cove-Temple litigation file. Then, if she had time, poke through his file on Buddy Todd. She'd like to know the nature of the meeting Buddy had with Dohnan. Sure, she could wait and ask Dohnan about it, but if Buddy was his client, he couldn't breach attorney-client privilege and tell her. If Buddy wasn't his client, he still wouldn't tell her after the way she'd treated him at The Lucky Duck.

She'd been intrigued at the coincidence of Dohnan's handling the case against her and meeting with Buddy Todd before his death. Then again, the number of lawyers practicing on the Cape was small. It could be just a coincidence.

Norma took a pen from the desk drawer. She felt uncomfortable sitting at Dohnan's desk, not because she'd gotten there under false pretenses. He deserved it and his receptionist should have prevented it. It was the desk picture of Dohnan and his wife that bugged her. They were gussied up for a banquet, doubtless an opportunity for Dohnan to make rain. What an apt term for the lawyer who brings big business to the firm. Someone like Dohnan brings plenty of rain to people's lives. She glared at his face in the picture and thought about other bald men she knew. Some men took no notice of their naked pate, others tried to hide it with a comb-over. The Dohnans of the world wore their baldness as a symbol of virility, like their pink dome was a giant glans with a smiley face.

"God, no wonder I'm single."

She settled down to her task. A half hour passed, and just as she was giving up on learning anything significant about the law suit against her she noticed a small manila folder, distinguished by its soft, greyed edges and a label that had probably been typed on an Olivetti. What made her heart race was the name on the label, Bradford C. Todd. What was that doing in the Cockle Cove-Temple litigation file? Couldn't have been misfiled by the receptionist. Must have been Dohnan himself who put it there, which was interesting.

Coigne had said Buddy's real name was Bradford. Was it possible Bradford C. Todd was the late lamented Buddy? She perused the file quickly, shuffling through a power of attorney, an old invoice, correspondence, and notes from phone calls. Nothing of interest there.

The receptionist popped his head in. "It's almost 5:00. Isn't that your deadline?"

"Thanks for the time, Big Ben."

"My name is Carl. And your name is?"

Her time was running out. She skimmed the next page.

Title Insurance
Insured: Bradford C. Todd.
Property: 212-216 Samoset Way
Red River, MA 02609

What the hell? Based on the title insurance, it looked like Laney's father owned property bordering Samoset Beach. She was sure that property was owned by Red River Resort. *And why was that file in the Cockle Cove Inn-Temple litigation file? Wait a minute. How could a "lowlife drifter," as Coigne described Buddy Todd, own that piece of property?* Then she remembered. Coigne had said the *family* had owned property but sold it off. Maybe Bradford C. Todd was Buddy's father.

Carl took a step closer to the desk. "Your name is...?"

"Just tell your boss 'Last Night' stopped by. He'll know." Norma winked. She hoped it would give Carl something to think about while she made her getaway.

Her car was so hot from sitting in the sun, Norma could barely breathe. A vague concern crept over her as she sped down Iyannough Road, gusts of hot air buffeting her through the four open windows. She might be disbarred for what she'd just done, or worse. These worries about the rules of professional ethics were soon replaced by a bigger one. She needed to make sure Laney was safe. What Coigne had said was right. Laney was somehow connected to everything, maybe even the lawsuit against Norma.

16

Laney regretted wearing beaded sandals for a bike ride, but sneakers would have made her sweaty feet smell. She was glad she'd stuffed a five-dollar bill in her pocket. If she was willing to pedal far enough she'd reach Postal I Scream, a new ice-cream place in an old post office building. It was right off the bike path. The cost was worth it in this heat and she wouldn't be depleting her stash that much. During the past six weeks she'd worked as a mother's helper for the weekly summer renters down the bluff. She'd slip a postcard with her phone number, address, age, experience and references in their screen door every Saturday, timing it just right—after the current renters and cleaning people left, but before the new renters arrived. The family staying this week had brought their own helper, which was fine because Laney wanted time off to spend with Aunt Norma during her staycation.

Making sure no one was coming in front or behind, she leaned over her handle bar and pumped her legs as fast as she could. Sitting upright, she lifted her hands up and coasted, the wind making her T-shirt bubble in the back. The warm air felt like it came from a blow dryer set on low. The trail down to Postal I Scream was right up ahead.

A soft hum made her glance over her shoulder and she caught sight of a biker hunched over his razor-thin bike, moving fast. He wore goggles and a helmet, and with his skintight red and blue bike suit he reminded her of a comic-book character.

She slowed and turned down the trail for ice cream.

People who lined up on the wide front steps of Postal I Scream were always smiling and gossiping and playing with their kids, but never fighting. Laney thought it was because ice cream was something that could be counted on to please everyone, from grandparents to toddlers, new friends and old neighbors, all those people who'd cram into a summer cottage by the sea. For Laney, the fun was in choosing outrageous flavor combinations—moose tracks and pistachio was her favorite. She'd limit herself to two scoops, but go wild on jimmies.

The steps were empty. Everyone must still be at the beach or getting ready for dinner, but someone was inside. She could hear "Y-M-C-A" playing on the juke-box.

Gran told her the shop had been a real post office once, but all that was left now were wide-plank floors, a wall-size bank of numbered boxes, each with a small glass window so the owner could see if there was mail inside, and a long wooden counter over the ice-cream case where Mr. Tremba handed out ice cream and collected money. She liked to study the boxes, hoping one day she might see a forgotten letter inside. She would have studied them today but instead froze at the screen door.

Isabella Miller sat facing the post office boxes, cone in hand, twirling her tongue around the tip of her ice cream. She was by herself. Laney stared as the dark-eyed girl now stuck the entire ice cream end of the cone into her mouth and pulled it out slowly, shaping the cool sweetness into a curl.

Laney felt her face burn. Her hands were stuck in midair, as though still pushing open the screen door. She wanted to turn around and go.

"Laney. Hi. Moose tracks. The *best.*"

"I was going to order moose tracks."

"Mr. Tremba's in the back. Get your ice cream and sit with me. I'll put on another song."

Laney's brain scrambled. *What can I talk about that isn't dumb?*

Mr. Tremba took her order. He always tried to sound cheerful, but his tall scrawny frame, sunken chest, and wisps of white hair made him look harassed and unhappy. While waiting for her order, Laney caught sight of her armpit sweat rings in the mirror behind the ice-cream case and wanted to die.

Cone in hand, she made her way to Isabella's table. For the next twenty minutes she listened, enthralled, as Isabella complained about how the summer was so boring, listed the courses she would take in the fall, and explained why she felt their English teacher was hot. Laney would have been in heaven if she hadn't been so tongue-tied. She had no gossip or small talk to offer. The best she could do was complain about how hot it was along the bike path and about the comic-book character she'd seen there.

"Did you hear about that guy who drowned on Samoset Beach? You live near there, don't you, Laney?

Haltingly Laney got the story out about finding the dead man. "The police say he was murdered."

"You found him? Why didn't you say so? Tell me everything."

Laney recounted the tale, leaving out nothing but her encounter with Sandal Man. The thought of explaining how she'd hidden under the table at the Red River Resort was too embarrassing.

Her moment in heaven ended all too soon. Two sets of parents and a knot of writhing children entered the shop, and behind them, Isabella's father. As she left she said, "Why don't you come over tomorrow, Laney?"

Did she really say that? Laney stared at the doorway after Isabella left and tried to remember exactly what she'd said.

The Village People brought Laney back to consciousness— she'd be humming "Y-M-C-A" for the rest of the day. But what a glorious day! She unlocked her bike in a trance, and almost didn't notice the comic-book character again, standing at the top of the trail. She'd called him Spider-Man for Isabella's benefit and even made her laugh. He was adjusting his goggles and his lithe figure blocked her way. She hesitated. He moved his bike to the side to let her pass.

She started heading east, but with the waning sunlight barely making it through the trees she changed her mind. When she turned around, the biker was practically on her rear wheel. They both braked fast. Straddling his bike, he nodded and smiled. His teeth looked so white next to his dark skin. It couldn't be.

The biker seemed to be talking to himself until she realized he was on a phone. "Now," she heard him say.

Laney gripped her handlebar. She heard wheels behind her.

The smiling biker looked over Laney's shoulder. He pulled his goggles down to his chin. "Please do not worry, Laney. No one will hurt you." His voice sounded like a lullaby, but his eyes were black stones. She had no more doubt. Spider-Man was Sandal Man. "You must come with us now," he soothed.

The wheels she'd heard a moment before stopped behind her. She turned. The other biker was looking at Sandal Man, waiting. She turned back around again slowly, then willed herself to go, go, go, popping a wheelie and propelling forward for dear life. As Sandal Man swung around to follow her, his wheel caught hers and he lost his balance.

She was frightened and her tears made it hard to see. The bike path was bordered on each side by steep declines, on one side thick woods, on the other, Marymac Pond. No choice— straight ahead, then back to Postal I Scream. Could she make that sharp turn at this speed without falling?

Voices behind her. They were catching up. No time to reach the trail. Laney swung her bike off the path and down the hill toward the pond. "Don't look back," she told herself. A branch smacked her face and barely missed her eye. She held on when her tire hit a rock. The ground turned soft closer to the pond and her front tire stuck. She ditched the bike, used her arms to thrash through the brush, and ran into the pond, dolphin diving as deep as she could go. Her sandals slowed her down, but she wouldn't stop to take them off.

She tried to calm herself, reasoning, *I'd hear them if they were in the water.* Then she realized, *No, my splashing drowns out their noise.* She surfaced and looked around without slowing her crawl stroke. *Was that a man in a kayak? How far away?* She dared to look behind her and spotted two men by the side of the pond, one bent over, removing his shoes, the other holding two bikes.

Her side ached. The kayak was moving away, the oar dipping from side to side, the boat gliding out of view. She treaded water. "Help!" The wind was against her. He couldn't hear her. "Help!" She started moving forward again. The kayak was slowing down and turning her way.

Laney looked back again. One man still holding the bikes, the other in the water.

17

Norma rounded the corner of Samoset Bluff Lane. A cruiser was parked in Anne's driveway. Norma parked on the street and stomped on the emergency brake, the violence of the movement relieving a little anxiety. They were probably following up on the murder investigation, that's all. Or maybe they were telling Gin about Ken Crawford's death. The fact that Coigne didn't mention these follow-up plans when she spoke with him an hour and a half ago shouldn't have surprised her. He wasn't going to give up information without getting something in return. She slammed the car door and tore across Anne's front yard.

What did surprise Norma was the living room tableau, two young, chubby-faced policemen staring at her, Anne standing stiff as a mummy, and most astonishing of all, Gin smoking a cigarette in Anne's pristine living room.

Gin reacted to Norma's arrival first. She didn't finish exhaling before speaking and the cigarette smoke weakened the force of her attack. "If Laney's with you, you sure as hell better have a good reason for keeping her out without calling us."

"That's a reasonable accusation, coming from Mother-of-the-Year." Norma wasn't taking any bullshit. "As a matter of fact, she's not with me, so let me ask *you*…." Her instinct for blasting any adversary made her almost miss the point. Laney wasn't where she was supposed to be. She turned for confirmation to Anne, who had backed against the curve of her baby grand, away from the fray. The grooves from her nose to the corners of her mouth seemed to have deepened in the last few hours.

"What's up, Anne. I take it no one's heard from Laney?"

"We were hoping she was with you," she said, her voice almost inaudible.

Norma nodded, trying to show there was no reason to get excited. "Where did she say she was going?"

Gin cut in. "She didn't say. She just took off. Not exactly considerate."

"Oh shut up, Gin!"

One of the policemen flinched at Anne's rebuke. Gin smashed her cigarette into a saucer.

The tug of war between Anne and Gin was too all-consuming for Norma to get their attention. She turned to the policemen, who looked like frightened twins. All they could add to the information she already had was that Ms. Sager had called 911 and they'd just arrived to take the report.

She had to reach Coigne. Only he fully understood the implications of Laney's disappearance and could commandeer the resources to find her.

Anne had turned her back to the group and was staring out the window toward the water. On any other occasion, the sun's disappearing act would have been the center of everyone's attention. Norma joined her and placed a hand on her shoulder.

"When you called earlier asking us to stay put," Anne said, "I thought Laney was upstairs. She must have left hours ago, when Gin and I were on the deck. Maybe I should have waited before calling the police, but she's never been gone so long. And what with everything on the beach yesterday . . ."

"She's fine, Anne. I'm sure she is."

Her friend crumpled and wept on Norma's shoulder. Anne had reason to worry, but Norma needed her to be clear-headed. She was relieved when her friend stopped crying.

"Oh, Norma, we behaved badly in front of her. That's probably why she left without saying anything. This is my fault."

"Cut it out, Anne. This is no time for self-recrimination." Anne's deteriorating condition made Norma realize everyone needed a job to do to keep them from tormenting themselves or one another.

She turned to Gin. "You stay by the landline. If anyone calls about Laney, you call me or Lieutenant Coigne, whoever you reach first." Norma read out his number from her cell phone. "Anne. Contact Laney's classmates and find out if anyone knows where she might be. Then call me or Coigne. I'm going out to look for her and I'll come back in a couple of hours. I'll leave the Tarleton Twins here with you in case Coigne wants them to do something."

Gin said, "I haven't heard from Kenny in a long time either."

Gin would be in for a rough time when she learned of Crawford's death, but Norma couldn't keep the brutality out of her voice. "Focus on your daughter for once."

She slid behind her wheel and checked her watch. Not yet 7:00 p.m. *Were they all overreacting?* Reflecting on her dog's dead body, to say nothing of two dead men, answered that question.

She pulled onto Route 28 and tried Coigne. No luck. While trying another number, she reviewed the scene she'd just left. Anne was normally the calm one, the personification of control in the face of adversity. Yet, in the last day or two she'd been almost remote, and even when she was in the present and paying attention she was irritable. Of course Norma hadn't had that much exposure to Anne in the bosom of her family. God, she'd hate for anyone to have seen her in the bosom of hers. She thought about her own parents. When she was young, a lot of kids at school pitied a girl named Sarah Winkler, whose parents had died in a plane crash. Norma didn't pity her, she envied her. But why think of that now?

Dusk. Impossible to see much along the road. At least traffic wasn't bad.

Anne's life had been different, enviable. She'd grown up in a posh suburb of New York City, a daughter of privilege. She'd floated through school winning all the prizes and then she'd married Milton Milquetoast, at least that's what he sounded like from Anne's description. But then, that seemed to be the worst that could be said about him. Why did she choose him? He was probably a good musician. Not as good as Anne, perhaps. Norma wasn't sure Anne would have married him if he had been. Another thing that puzzled Norma was how their offspring, little Gin, had turned out to be so whacked. Norma occasionally considered telling Anne to ease up on Gin. The girl was doing the best she could with what she had. But who was Norma to criticize? She'd only raised a dog and had let him down when he needed her most.

She finally reached Coigne. They agreed to meet in the parking lot of Sidney's Diner, a greasy spoon whose year-round popularity defied explanation. Its mid-century counter stools were always filled to overlapping with 21st century behinds. Sidney's was in West Nauset. That was something that bugged her about the Cape. She could find no correlation between the points on a compass and names of the towns. West Nauset wasn't in the western part of Nauset, nor was it west of East Nauset. Good thing she knew the way to Sydney's.

Coigne's cruiser must have had a jet engine. His and two others idled in the empty lot as she pulled up.

He walked over and she tried to calibrate his level of concern. Not that she intended to rely on his assessment of the situation. She just wanted to know.

"We've put out an Amber Alert and I just heard from Ms. Sager with an update on what Laney was wearing. She must have changed her clothes before going out. Everyone's getting briefed."

"Good information." Norma was relieved Anne was using her head now.

"I've also learned from her that a girlfriend saw Laney this afternoon. They met at Postal I Scream, just down the road off the bike path. And Laney had her bike. That might help locate her. We're searching the bike path while there's still some light." He checked his notepad. "I'm going to meet with the girlfriend and her family. Isabella Miller. She lives back in Red River. You want to come? She might feel more at ease if you're there."

Norma frowned. She wasn't known for putting people at ease, but detected no sarcasm in his voice.

"Well?" He stood with his hand on her car door handle.

"Let's go." She grabbed an oil-stained sweatshirt from her backseat.

Off-Cape, you'd call the Miller home a modest townhouse. On the Cape you called it a Water View and put a million-dollar price tag on it.

Mr. Miller met them at the door after one knock. With him came a gust of air conditioning scented with air freshener. He might have been good-looking with his deep-set, intelligent eyes, but Norma couldn't see beyond his hard expression. He offered no greeting, just ushered them into the living room. It looked like a page torn from a coastal travel magazine—white walls, white furnishings, pastel accents, nautical paintings, no personal items of any kind. Mrs. Miller stood to greet them. When she resumed her seat her thighs didn't splay one centimeter. Norma guessed she worked out and wasn't a regular at Sydney's.

The girl beside Mrs. Miller was a budding stunner. Isabella's dark hair was pulled back from her face, uncovering a widow's peak and framing her dad's dark eyes. But her wide, generous smile, full of innocent mischief, was all her own.

She gave them a detailed description of Laney's clothing, reconstructed precisely what the girls had talked about and asked if she could join the search, a request her father immediately squelched.

Norma thought, *Isabella's a good friend for Laney to have.* She also reluctantly admitted she was impressed with the way Coigne was handling the interview.

He said, "Anything else you remember? Anything that might tell us the direction she was heading in?"

Isabella hesitated. Norma willed her to think of something solid that would help. When she finally spoke, it was to say a name. "Spider-Man."

"What are you talking about, Isabella?"

The girl ignored her father's rude tone. "I doubt it helps, but she joked about a biker she saw on the bike path. She called him Spider-Man."

"It was probably just some kid," Miller said.

"What do *you* think, Isabella?"

"Laney didn't say one way or the other, Lieutenant Coigne. But I figure if it was a kid, she would have known who it was and used his name."

Norma had an idea. "What exactly did she say about Spider-Man? Think of her exact words if you can."

"It's kind of silly, the way it came out. She said, 'Ice cream hits the spot, when you're hot.' We laughed at the rhyme and I said, 'Especially at five on the dot,' and we went on like that. Then she said she sure was hot from biking, but nothing like Spider-Man, this guy she saw on the bike path who was wearing a long-sleeved bike suit. So now that I think about it, if it was a kid, she would have said kid, not guy."

Miller, standing all this time with hands in his pockets, shrugged. "You can't draw conclusions."

Mrs. Miller sat ramrod straight and took no part in the conversation.

"Why would anyone wear such an outfit? Do you think it might have been one of those guys who delivers balloons on birthdays?" Coigne directed his question to everyone.

"Could be, but she'd have mentioned balloons," Norma said. "No, if I know Laney, she called him Spider-Man as a shorthanded way of describing his appearance—his biking attire. It was a kidding kind of shorthand, something she had a habit of doing to describe people." She added to Coigne in a low voice, "Like Sandal Man."

Isabella clapped in excitement. "If she was describing his biking suit and called him Spider-Man, it must have been red and blue, with goggles maybe."

"You weren't there when she saw him, Isabella. Keep quiet." Miller must have heard the harshness in his voice. "These people need facts, honey, not guesses."

"But that's the way Laney talks. It's funny. That's one of the reasons I like her," she said to Norma.

Thank you, dear, for ignoring your bonehead father. Norma hoped she'd just thought that and not said it out loud.

Coigne stood. "I think we've kept you up long enough, Isabella."

"You'll let us know, won't you, Lieutenant? If you hear anything?" Mrs. Miller had decided to join the conversation as they left the room.

"Of course."

They stepped outside and Norma breathed deeply. "This close to the water, you'd think they'd open the window and breathe salt air." She leaned against the cruiser door. The moths were out with a vengeance, pinging against the amber street light.

Coigne was still thinking over the interview. "Why would anyone wear that kind of gear on a scorcher like today?"

"Either the guy's in training for the Tour de France and has absolutely nothing to do with Laney or...he wore the gear to disguise himself."

"Because otherwise Laney would recognize him. Sandal Man?"

"I don't want to believe it, but we have to consider it. Where does that get us?"

Coigne's cell phone, still on vibrate after the interview, started moaning. "It tells us we need an all-points bulletin out on a dark-skinned, foreign-sounding guy in good shape, *and* we get more information about him from Gin and Anne. They saw him this morning. They have to know more than they've told us."

Coigne took his call and Norma waited. She wanted to join the police on the bike path.

"Hold on, Trooper, got another call coming in." Coigne held the phone away and squinted at it, then pressed a button. As he listened to his call, Norma watched his slack posture straighten and a look of concentration overtake his normally relaxed features.

"Go on." He turned his back to Norma. When he put his phone in his pocket and turned to face her, she knew something bad had happened.

"Tell me, Coigne."

"They found her bike. They found some other signs that she went into Marymac Pond."

"Don't say it, Coigne. Do not tell me they found a body."

"They did, Norma. No—wait. It was a man. They found his kayak."

"Drowned?"

"Yes."

18

Laney couldn't stop shaking. The man who'd hauled her out of the pond dragged her up a hill through the woods to the roadside. Whenever headlights appeared, he'd take a quick look, then yank her back into the woods, his hand pressed against her mouth. They waited.

He was a giant. His hair was long and once it dried it turned white-blond and curly like a girl's. His lips were full and red and he spoke only in two-word sentences like, "Shut up" and "Keep still."

The giant was worse than any of her mom's boyfriends. *What if he beats me up and rapes me.* She started to cry and covered the man's hand in tears and mucous.

"Aw shit!"

They must be waiting for Sandal Man. She was sure that's who chased her on the bike path.

A car sped their way. The giant leaned far out into the road, dragging Laney with him. She held her breath. It could be the police looking for her. Before it passed he'd pulled her back. The car's tail lights winked out of sight.

"Don't move."

Another car approached, headlights off. It pulled to the side of the road. Black Escalade, like Wheezy Wickersham had. She'd have to remember that. The giant shoved her in the back seat and jumped in.

The driver was not someone she recognized. His clothes were dry, unlike the giant's. The men mumbled to each other. The car swerved to avoid hitting something and they turned onto a gravel road. She thought about jumping out of the car and running, but she'd have to get through the thick woods surrounding them. Her hand crept toward the door handle. Click. The driver had locked her door from the front seat.

Despite the loud popping of gravel against the tires, bits of the men's conversation reached her. "Happened to Crawford," and "man in the kayak."

She remembered the look of surprise on the kayak owner's face when he finally heard her cry out. He'd looked all around and must have seen the giant swimming after her. She'd dived in deep again and headed underwater for the kayak. When she came up for air, the giant had changed course and was heading for the kayak too. Her arms were about to give out, but to escape the giant, she'd swum toward the far shore.

She'd heard the man say, "Hey, what do you think you're doing?" The giant must have tipped him over because she saw his paddle flip into the air. By the time she reached land, the giant had caught up to her. He'd grabbed her around her waist and run her into the woods like a football.

Huddled at the end of the gravel road was a dimly lit cottage. But for that light, all around was darkness. No moonlight or stars. And it was silent. No lapping waves or chirping crickets, just their own car doors slamming.

She was hungry, wet and cold, but another need was more urgent. "I need to use the bathroom."

"Too bad."

She didn't think she could hold it.

His voice rose as he pushed her forward toward the cottage. "Get moving."

"Jeez, Varn. Relax for God's sake." The driver shook his head.

"*You* relax."

If only she'd not gone for a bike ride and stayed home. The thought of Gran and her mom made her cry again.

They mounted the front steps onto a screen porch, then moved into a tiny living room. An overhead lightbulb shone on soiled upholstered chairs that may have once been blue, matching the wall-to-wall carpeting. The giant, Varn, pushed her toward the back of the house and into the kitchen. A ceramic lighthouse lamp on the counter was the only light in the room. The floor was covered in torn green linoleum, sticky beneath her shoes. A trash can was filled to overflowing with Domino's Pizza boxes and beer cans. Without a word, Varn opened the door to a closet and pushed her in.

"Don't! Please don't shut the door." She leaned hard against it, but Varn's violent shove against her made her lose her balance and fall back. Twisting the doorknob did no good.

She felt for a wall light switch, then waved her arms through the air in search of a string. Nothing. The glow from the lighthouse lamp seeped under the door. Her eyes started to adjust. She was in a deep pantry, twice the size of a closet. The shelves were empty. A short broom was propped in the corner. She crossed her legs tightly and began counting. When she reached two hundred a car door slammed. Footsteps on the stairs. Muffled voices.

"Where is she?"

Sandal Man! She started to pee. Ignoring the warning from Varn she banged on the door. "I need to use the bathroom."

"That's it," Varn said.

"Calm yourself, Mr. Varn. Tony, show her to the ladies' room. Then bring her here. If you please."

When Tony, the driver, opened the bathroom door for her, the stench made them both rear back. In the toilet, a cigarette butt floated in foamy urine. She could hear Tony breathing outside the door as he waited for her. She was past caring.

Sandal Man pointed toward the living room. At some point he had changed from his biking gear into a tan business suit. "At last, we can have our little chat. You've caused me some trouble, you know, but you may yet make it worth my while." He smiled. "Let us hope so."

"Why am I here?"

He motioned her to a chair. "First things first. My name is Mr. Singh—yes, like sing a song, but with an H. To answer your question, you are here because of who you are, who your family is, and what you know."

Laney could not have been more surprised. She'd never felt that who she was could matter to anyone. In her own mind, her background was shameful. *And what was she supposed to know? She was thirteen.*

"Your father told you about something before he drowned. It was a letter." He leaned forward, as though he'd given her a big hint and now it was her turn.

She could only stare. Then hope flooded her. "You have made a mistake, Mr. Singh. You have the wrong person. I don't know my father."

For a moment he didn't speak. "I see. The fact that you live five miles from the hotel where he's been living for months is a coincidence. The fact that you found his body is also a coincidence. But you don't want to admit this. I see." He kept nodding. His words were neutral, even gentle, but his face was angry.

"I'm telling the truth." Laney wanted to convince him, but she was also afraid of disappointing him.

"Varn!" All trace of Mr. Singh's polite voice was gone.

19

Norma fought back despair. A man had been drowned, right where Laney's bike was found. Sandal Man would stop at nothing.

Coigne had driven her to the diner parking lot where she'd left her car and gotten out with her. She thought he was going to tell her his next move in the investigation. Instead he opened her car door and looked at her, his forehead creased and his eyes questioning. For a second she was confused.

He placed a hand on her shoulder. "The best thing you can do now—"

"I don't need advice." She brushed his hand off like it was a bug. "I need you to do your job." She got in her car and drove off. Without knowing her own next move in the search, she headed to Samoset Beach to think about it.

Standing in the sand where the horror began just the day before brought neither inspiration nor solace. *I can stand here and listen to waves lapping or get a move on,* she thought. What she refused to do was wonder why she had snapped at Coigne. There was no time and besides, did it matter? She answered her own question in the affirmative. It hadn't escaped her notice that he was now telling her far more than he needed to and even including her in that interview. He might get angry enough to exclude her from further involvement. She also felt something disturbing after her show of temper—remorse. She wasn't sure Coigne deserved quite so much disrespect as she was dishing out. But as with other inklings that caused her to reconsider strong positions taken, she tossed this inkling away with a comforting and dispositive, "Whatever."

By now, the police would have told Anne about finding Laney's bike at Marymac Pond, maybe even told her of the drowned man with the kayak. Despite overwhelming fatigue, she stopped by Anne's to offer support.

Her friend was playing the piano, one of Chopin's Ballades. Norma didn't interrupt, but stood in the doorway until the sound died. Anne's fingers lingered over the keys and she studied them, as though waiting for what they might play next.

Norma wasn't sure Anne knew she'd arrived until she shifted around on the piano bench and said, "I've just heard from Lieutenant Coigne."

Norma nodded and sat down. Anne told her what she'd learned, then said, "When you called earlier today, you said you wanted to talk about something. What was it?"

"You feel up to it? You look like hell."

"Go ahead."

"Buddy Todd. All these years, I thought no one knew who Laney's father was. You never mentioned him. Why?"

"I'm sorry I didn't tell you about him, Norma, but really, to know him was to want to forget him and believe me, I tried hard." Anne left the piano and sat down in the armchair across from Norma. "Lieutenant Coigne's description of Buddy as a low-life drifter was kind. Compared to him, Gin *was* Mother-of-the-Year. He was no ordinary heroin addict—he was the bad kind you see in documentaries who sacrifice anything and anyone, including their children, to feed their habit."

Norma said nothing. She couldn't imagine what it was like for Anne to know Laney's father was a monster.

"Gin's upstairs by the way, coping with the news about Crawford's death. Probably took something to calm down. Helpful, right?" Anne couldn't resist adding.

Norma didn't want the conversation to devolve into a Gin-bash. Anne needed hope and resilience, but all the life and intelligence that usually radiated from her face had drained away, leaving behind a frail, old woman. "The police are pretty certain Laney's "Sandal Man" is involved in her disappearance. If you still don't remember any more about him, Anne, maybe Gin will."

"Gin doesn't retain information that long. I'm afraid talking to her would be a waste of time."

If Gin had taken a pill "to calm down," Anne was probably right. Norma would try her in a few hours. In the meantime, she brought Anne a glass of sherry and left.

Her house was quiet, making Norma relive her loss. Bark wasn't there to leap at her and convey all that love through his slobbering pounce. "He's lying on a slab, dead. Deal with it."

Her spirits sank further at the sight of her once comfortable home. Coigne's men had poked around looking for evidence. They'd called in a hauling company to help her get rid of the broken glass, bed stuffing, and other things beyond repair. It was up to Norma to sort through salvageable items like scratched furniture, scattered clothes and torn books. Her head throbbed, trying to figure out where to begin, but it didn't matter anyway. Straightening up wasn't her priority.

Norma had gotten through law school by avoiding subjects that bewildered her and working like hell on those she could master. She'd use that strategy now. Coigne was in the best position to follow up on most leads, but there was one in her sole possession, which she'd picked up at Dunscombe and Dohnan. She needed to understand how the Todd family's ownership of that slip of property on Samoset Way fit in with everything else that had happened, especially Laney's disappearance.

She grabbed a yellow legal pad and on a clean sheet, titled it "Facts" and started a list.

1. Laney Sager meets Sandal Man at beach, discovers Buddy Todd's body. Buddy was on his way to lawyer Dohnan, angry and with proof of paternity.

2. I get notice of lawsuit involving Mary Temple's sale of her Red River Resort interest to other Red River Resort partners.

3. Gin Sager pops up, transformed from slag to debutante, demanding custody of Laney.

4. Gin accompanied by fiancé (Crawford), partner in Red River Resort, which is current owner of Samoset Way property.

5. I get beaten up and my house trashed by caller who mentions Laney/beach drowning.

6. Laney sees Sandal Man at Red River Resort. Crawford knows Sandal Man.

7. Crawford murdered.

8. Buddy Todd's father (?) was represented by attorney Dohnan in the sale of Samoset Way land to Red River Resort.

9. Laney kidnapped.

10. Based on Isabella Miller interview, Sandal Man preliminarily identified as kidnapper.

11. Laney's bike found near Marymac Pond. Man in kayak on Pond drowned—collateral damage?

Norma traced her finger down the list. "Okay, now what?"

She flipped through the hard copy of her Inn at Cockle Cove file. As she'd told the police, her computer and hard drive had been destroyed, but since she kept an external hard drive in her safe deposit box and updated it quarterly, her practice wasn't completely destroyed. It would still be a pain to restore what she'd lost.

She started with the subfile labeled Correspondence. Most of the time she reveled in rereading her letters to obnoxious lawyers because of her flair for mudslinging invective. This set of letters was mild and boring, but she forced herself to read every one.

It was past 1:00 a.m. when she finished reading her entire Inn at Cockle Cove file. The hum of a passing car reminded her of life outside. Some people were actually enjoying a vacation on the Cape. She thought of the last time she'd gone clamming with Laney, which made her picture the girl frantically swimming away from Sandal Man. She blocked the thought.

Norma never had a desire to have children and on meeting Laney that first time, she'd barely nodded at the shy girl. How freakish she'd seemed with all that blinking. And she'd been aggravated that Anne's time would be consumed by her new charge. Soon she noticed Laney paid close attention to her every word and asked questions, good ones, nonstop. She followed Norma everywhere, although the attraction was probably Bark. Norma saw Laney as a misfit, like herself, but even misfits have dreams that shouldn't be crushed, especially not by their parents. Eventually Norma sought Laney out, took her sailing, brought her to baseball games. She even invited her to summer evening band concerts, events her musically discriminating Gran refused to attend. But thinking like this was getting her nowhere.

Norma summarized what she'd learned by mastering her file. There was nothing in the file out of order, incorrect, no smoking gun, not even a tempting red herring to follow, yet instinct told her clues to the murders and Laney's disappearance were in that file.

20

The phone rang. Norma recognized the number and picked up.

"You found her, Coigne?"

"No. I—"

"You're calling me at 2:00 a.m. to tell me what?" Norma heard the sound of her own voice and remembered Coigne was her lifeline to information. "Sorry. Go ahead."

"It's about Crawford. I looked over the search report of his house. Found a fair amount of photos and biographical information on Gin and Laney. There were also some interesting emails between the couple."

"He planned to marry the woman. What's your point?"

Coigne drew in his breath and exhaled slowly.

"Sorry," she said.

"My point is this. I had the impression from everyone's reaction that Crawford and Gin Sager had only recently met and started a courtship. The emails tell a different story. They rekindled a romance that had started and ended in their teens. Looks like Crawford called her about six months ago. Before that, they'd had no contact for fourteen, fifteen years."

"Hm. About the time she was on the Cape as a teen with her mother."

"The biographical information was compiled in a report by a local PI, Leonard Diamond. Works with the law firm Buchanan and Associates. Know him?"

"Never heard of him. I rarely use PIs. I know the Buchanan firm, though. You say it was information on Gin *and* Laney?"

"That's right."

"Anything there we didn't already know?"

"Not really."

No one spoke for a moment.

"I guess you called me because you'd like my opinion. If not, you're getting it anyway," Norma said. "Our working theory is that Crawford's death is tied to Buddy Todd's and Sandal Man is behind it all, including the vandalizing of my home. I don't know how significant the documents are that you found, but it would have been an easy matter for Sandal Man to find and destroy them if they're important. Look at what happened at my house. But if the documents aren't all that important, maybe what is significant is the timing of the report and the rekindling of romance between Crawford and Gin."

"What do you mean?"

"You said there was bio information on Laney. You've got Crawford and Gin demanding custody of Laney. Meanwhile, Buddy Todd is running around with DNA evidence in his pocket proving he's Laney's father. He's a drifter. How long has he been on the Cape?"

"He'd been staying at the Skaket Seaside Hotel about seven months."

"Where was he before that?"

"Rehab in Philadelphia."

"Then I'd say his discharge from rehab set a ball in motion. Suddenly everyone wants Laney. We just need to find out what that "ball" was, where Buddy went, who he talked to. What have you gotten out of the lawyer he was going to see, Derek Dohnan?"

"Nothing. He says he has no idea why Buddy wanted to meet with him, just that Todd said it was very important."

"Okay, that's bullshit." Norma told Coigne about the history of ownership of Samoset Way and the fact that Derek Dohnan represented Buddy Todd's relative, probably his father, in its sale to Red River Resort. Coigne agreed the fact that Buddy and Crawford had ties to the same property, and were suddenly dead, was unusual. She also told him she'd just been sued over the sale of her client's interest in the resort and Derek Dohnan represented the guys who were suing her, the Temple brothers. She skipped the part about reviewing the files at the offices of Dunscombe and Dohnan.

Coigne asked, "Where exactly is this property?"

Norma told him.

"You mean that strip right by the beach?"

"Yes, same beach where Buddy Todd's body was found."

"I wasn't thinking about that so much. After the last three hurricanes, that strip is the only land access to the beach. Red River Resort lets the neighborhood use it."

"I know that. I live here."

"What you may not know, Norma, is that the resort has recently threatened to end the neighbors' access."

"Why? Surely they can't build on it. It's too close to the marsh."

"They don't want to build on it. Don't you read your local paper? They're using the land "card" to persuade the neighbors to support them in their bid to develop other property nearby."

"Of course. If the neighbors, as abutters, object to the development, Red River Resort will get tied up in knots with the Zoning Board and litigation, meanwhile losing their financing and their development plan goes kaput. To ward off the abutter threat, the resort quietly threatens to end the neighbors' right of way. Is that it?"

Coigne yawned. "You got it."

"But do the neighbors really care about more development? This whole area has gone from quiet fishing village to Miami Beach in a couple of decades."

"That's a slight exaggeration, Norma. But what Red River Resort has in mind is much bigger and more profitable than any previous development. It's going to be some sort of exclusive fortification for the rich and famous, with housing, shopping, theaters, parks, the works. They'll include a state-of-the-art spa, the one feature their flagship lacks, and it hurts them bigtime."

"All that right here? But that's outrageous. This will make the wind farm controversy look like small potatoes. Tater tots."

"What no one knows is where all the money is coming from for a project like that. Red River Resort is doing well, they say, but for that kind of project we're talking megabucks."

"That rings a bell. When I was handling Mary Temple's sale of her resort interest, there was some foreign investor who funded their purchase of it. Could be that's where the money for the development's coming from. Anyway, you've convinced me that property is valuable as a means to an end for the resort. But where does that get us?"

"It gets us headed in a new direction. You sound exhausted. You okay there by yourself?"

"What, you moving in?"

"Good night, Norma."

Norma plodded to the bathroom to wash up. In the mirror, bloodshot eyes stared back at her. *Is it possible Coigne's attracted to me?* No. She was too big in all respects—from the size of her feet to the limitless boundaries of her ego. She stretched out on her now three-legged sofa and thought of Laney. It had been awhile since she'd said a prayer, but she said one now.

21

Varn pounded up the front steps. "She ready?"

Mr. Singh held his arm out toward Laney, palm up. "Be my guest."

Laney shrank from Varn like he was poisonous gas. He grabbed her by the hair, making her cry out. "That's nothing," he said. He pushed her toward the front door and kicked her backside, making her fall through the screen and onto all fours.

"Varn, please. You know you are not permitted to hurt young people where I can hear you." Mr. Singh closed the door behind them.

Laney rose, her fear giving way to anger.

"No use you screamin'." Varn pushed her down the steps and she rolled into the drive. This time, she stayed where she was. Varn clutched the back of her T-shirt and prodded her toward the woods.

"One reason no use screamin', no one'll hear you in the woods. N'other, noise bothers me, like it bothers the boss. You cry again, I cut your tongue out." To show her he meant business, he flashed a switch blade in her face.

"You cut my tongue out, Mr. Singh won't get what he needs from me. Then he'll cut *your* tongue out."

Varn looked stunned, but the surprise at her insolence didn't last. He whipped her around and swung a mad backhand across her face, knocking her down.

She didn't feel pain, just blood pooling in her mouth. Her mind focused on one thing. She rose slowly, protective of the ammunition now in hand.

Varn resumed their march into the woods. "Move on."

Her slow pace was intended to show submission and resignation. As they got farther from the cottage, they were in complete darkness. Varn told her to stay still as he lit a match. He said, "What's that?"

She stared straight ahead, as though she didn't hear him.

"I said what's in your hand?" He moved toward her.

"Take a look."

She held her hand just out of reach and he moved closer. She flung her handful of sand and gravel into his eyes and took off.

"Bitch!" he yelled, but swallowed the word and stumbled after her.

She was almost running blind herself, but took heart. If the darkness and sharp pine branches slowed her down, they'd be much harder on a fat, wheezing giant with grit in his eyes.

Her ruse had worked and Laney silently thanked Aunt Norma for the idea. She'd once overheard Norma explaining to Gran, "I call the strategy Cupid's Revenge. You talk sweet while opposing counsel beats you to a pulp. Then, when he thinks you're done for and he's taking his bow before the jury, you shove a poison-tipped arrow right up his ass." Her handful of sand and gravel had been her poison-tipped arrow. She would have smiled if she weren't so frightened.

Judging by the sound of Varn's gasps, she knew he was moving in a zigzag pattern, stopping to listen every so often, maybe clearing his eyes. He was a couple of hundred yards away. *What will he do?* He might go back and get help, or if he didn't want Mr. Singh to know he'd lost her, he'd keep running after her. No matter what, Mr. Singh would be looking for him, and her, soon.

The woods offered Laney plenty of trees to climb, but if Varn found her, she'd be trapped. And he would find her. The pine needles screamed beneath her sandals. Once more she cursed herself for wearing flimsy sandals on a bike ride to get ice cream. Ice cream. It seemed so long ago.

She had a general idea how to reach the main road they'd turned off. If she just had more distance from Varn, she might be able to get there before he caught up.

But he was gaining on her. No choice but to take a chance and climb. She jumped to grasp the lowest branch and keeping her arms apart, stuck her legs between them and hung upside down until Varn stopped running. When he resumed, she released one leg and hurled her torso over the limb. Her arms and legs were bleeding. She kept her eyes closed to protect them. They were useless in the dark anyway.

At the top of the tree she listened. Now he was very close. She permitted herself a small smile of triumph. He'd run past the tree and was heading away from the main road. She waited before climbing down, then jumped to the ground and took off in the opposite direction.

She thought she'd been running for about half an hour when she realized Varn's tread had been replaced by a different sound, the whoosh of tires on pavement.

Instinct kept her from jumping out into the road right away. She considered how she might look to a stranger—dirty shirt, torn and soaked with sweat, and bloodied face and limbs. Frightful, but it couldn't be helped.

At last, headlights. The road was hilly and its dips made the faraway glow appear, then disappear. She crept out of the woods, peering left and right. Salvation? The car dipped out of sight again.

A rustle from behind. The noise grew louder. "Please be a squirrel," she prayed. Heavy breathing. It had to be Varn.

She zoomed across the road. The car appeared again. It was getting close. By its lights she could see Varn step out of the woods where she'd been waiting. He could see right where she was, yet he didn't cross the road.

As the car neared, she realized it wasn't the Escalade. Laney jumped into the road, arms in a V. "Stop!"

The car slowed and turned toward her. She tried to see inside but was blinded by the headlights. The car backed up, gunned its engine and rolled forward.

22

Norma's home-office line pierced her REM sleep like a fire alarm. She ran to answer it and fumbled trying to get the receiver to her ear.

"And I could have you disbarred."

"And I could have you dismembered for calling me this early. Why are you calling, Dohnan?"

"You know damn well why. I've had a busy morning, Norma, firing my receptionist of seven years, getting him the hell out of the building without strangling him first, and restoring my office to order."

"I don't know what you're talking about."

"You know damn well you misrepresented yourself to gain access to my files. It's completely unethical for counsel to go through opposing counsel's litigation file."

"First of all, ass-wipe, I'm a party, not counsel." Okay, splitting hairs, and beside the point. "And second of all, I still don't know what you're talking about."

"Fine. I can have Carl identify you from a picture and let the police sort it out."

"And I can tell your wife I saw you and Bitty "Booty" Buchanan stroll into a Marriott hotel room and let her sort it out."

Norma congratulated herself on quick thinking after only a couple of hours' sleep. She'd have to thank Coigne for mentioning the Buchanan firm last night, which had made her remember the last time she was in Boston for a bar conference.

She'd spotted Dohnan and Bitty Buchanan, president of the Bar Association. *Hadn't they ever heard of a No-tell Motel?*

"I'm warning you, Norma. You'll be sorry."

"Kiss my—"

Click.

Good old Bitty "Booty" Buchanan, principal of Buchanan and Associates. Norma first met Bitty early in their careers at the Boston law firm Norma left after only one year. She remembered one incident that had told her all she needed to know about Bitty. Another young lawyer at the firm, a friend, Faith Benton, was asked to brief a major client of the firm on the status of a large class-action suit. Norma knew Faith was excited and apprehensive about the assignment. She prepared for hours and rehearsed her presentation with Norma and asked her to attend for moral support.

Bitty, one of the older lawyers on the case, was asked by a senior partner also to attend the briefing to support Faith. Within the first five minutes of Faith's presentation, Bitty lassoed the briefing away and never stopped talking until the ordeal ended. And thank God it did, as Faith looked stupefied and teary for its duration.

At the end of the session, Bitty justified herself to Faith. She'd felt compelled to take over as the firm couldn't afford to have the client misunderstand any aspect of the case. Bitty hadn't actually said, "You are too dumb to have been given the assignment and, in fact, too dumb for this firm." But even Norma, all of twenty-five, had gotten that message.

Norma had always hoped the day would come when Bitty would get her comeuppance, but so far she'd remained on an upward trajectory, looking down on the likes of Faith Benton, and Norma was certain, of Norma Bergen as well.

The thrust and parry with Dohnan would have been an invigorating diversion but Norma could think only of Laney. Her first order of business was to talk to Gin and grill her on what she remembered about Sandal Man.

Anne's house faced east. The morning sun burnished the graceful curves of her baby grand. The cheerful sight struck Norma as mockery.

She found Anne in the kitchen emptying her dishwasher. Anne said she'd been summoned to Skaket to try to identify Sandal Man from mug shots.

"Good. Action. How about Gin? She going too?"

Anne shook her head.

To Norma, her best friend looked like a stranger. More disconcerting than the uncombed hair and slumped shoulders was the trembling in her voice. Norma asked, "Do you know why she isn't going?"

"Too groggy to get up." Anne described the sideshow of the night before, giving Norma the impression Gin had taken enough pills to supply CVS for a month.

"Her own daughter's been kidnapped and she's too tired to get up?"

"If you want to give it a try, Norma, I'd be grateful. I can't stand another minute with her, God help me." Anne dried her hands and prepared to leave.

Norma took the stairs two at a time and, stepping into the hall bathroom, turned on the shower's cold spigot. She flung open the guest room door and, finding Gin curled into a ball, tore back the bedclothes, grabbed the deadweight and hauled her into the bathroom.

"Hey! Wah?"

With her free arm, Norma swept back the shower curtain.

"What's going—?"

"There you go, princess." Norma shoved her into the shower and, once certain Gin wouldn't fall and crack her skull, held the curtain tight at both ends to prevent her from exiting.

Gin's string of insults was the human function variety: "You're puke! You're a shit!" It confirmed Norma's belief that Gin had no imagination. No wonder Anne was disappointed.

She tossed Gin a towel. "There. Feeling refreshed?" With an arm around her waist, Norma hurried her back to the bedroom. On the way, Norma decided on a plan. She would get more useful information if she removed Gin from her mother's home and took her someplace that might jog her memory of recent events. "Get dressed. I'm taking you to Red River Resort."

"You're going like that?"

Norma considered her attire. She thought her consignment shop pedal pushers and white camp blouse, tinged pink from close association with a cheap red T-shirt in the wash, looked just right. "I won't embarrass you, Gin, not unless I have to. Now let's go."

Norma knew the grand hotel was always booked during peak season, yet there never seemed to be more than two or three guests in the cavernous lobby. They always looked like walk-ons in a play, drifting in from stage right and disappearing stage left. It amused her now to see a corporate type making the crossing, hair neatly trimmed but with his tennis shoes rakishly untied to suggest the turbulent inner man.

Gin had remained silent during the car ride, but now that they were in the lobby, wouldn't shut up. Norma only tuned in when she said, "It's impossible that Kenny and I were here just two days ago. Now he's gone and Laney's gone. Here today, gone tomorrow."

Norma yanked Gin around so fast she stumbled, then pulled her up so they faced each other, nose to nose. "Look, dumbbell, if you think for one moment I'm going to let you write Laney off, think again. You're going to help find her and if I meet with one second of resistance, I'll call on a friend of mine. Ex-con. Trained as a short-order cook. Used a paring knife on his girlfriend's face."

There was no such person, but Norma would be damned if she'd tolerate the idiot's apparent ennui at a time when Laney's life. She shut down that thought. The maître d' seated them at a table in a corner where there was no view and no other distraction, as Norma had requested. It was not quite lunchtime so they practically had the place to themselves.

She had to play it smart and let Gin suspect she already knew everything, so there would be no point in lying or hiding information. "You should know the police think your boyfriend's death is related to Laney's disappearance, so I want to know everything about him. Leave nothing out. Start with how you two met."

"Who do you think you are, the police? I don't have to answer you."

"Would you rather talk to the police?" Norma leaned forward and pulled her phone out of her back pocket. She punched two buttons, saying to Gin, "Speed dial," and waved the phone at her. "Go on, take it." This was a familiar trick on cop shows, but Norma figured Gin would fall for it.

Gin bobbled her head and rolled her eyes in theatrical resignation. "All right I'll tell you. A few months ago I came up to see Laney. Kenny saw me at a bar. He liked what he saw. He picked me up. That a crime?"

"That's the last lie you're going to tell me. I know you and Kenny met years ago and you were more than just friends. He contacted you again six months ago."

"If you know the truth, why are you asking?" Gin crossed her arms and leaned back, as if gloating over her masterful counterpunch.

The waiter arrived. He looked Norma over, shook his head, took their order, and left.

Norma started in again. "I know you two corresponded by email and text, Gin. Thousands of messages. A forensics team is studying them."

If Gin was like the rest of the world, she'd said things over the Internet she shouldn't have and hadn't a clue what those things were. Her sudden pallor confirmed Norma's hunch.

"We know what was going on. It would be better for you if you explained why. It may help in the long run."

Gin's eyes shifted left, then right. A poker player she'd never be.

"I had every right to Laney's property. And so did Kenny. He'd paid Old Man Todd good money for it."

Whoa. Norma hadn't seen that one coming, but did her best to sound like she had. "Right, go on, *Laney* had land that Ken Crawford bought from Old Man Todd."

"You know what I mean, that land she was supposed to inherit from her grandfather, at least.... Hey, I thought you said you knew everything." A thought must have then occurred to

Gin. The soft clink of silver, fine china and crystal filled the dead air. In a child's voice she asked, "Does my mother know about all this?"

23

Every year a local church held a "Blessing of the Fleet" to seek protection for the seamen and a good catch for the village. The gathered families and well-wishers would conclude the ceremony by picking a child to stand on the end of the dock and toss a decorative wreath out to sea. As surely as tides ebb and flow, the wreath landed upside down and crashed on the rocks. Norma envisioned just such a fate for Gin. The idea that Gin had tried to cheat her own daughter out of a possible inheritance made Norma want to hurl her through the window and out to sea.

All these years Norma had harbored a suspicion that Anne overstated her daughter's selfishness, and if Anne would only be more understanding of her daughter's inadequacies, the young woman might become a better person. But Norma knew the truth now. Gin was terminally rotten.

She wondered whether there was any difference between selling your kid for cash and doing what Gin and Crawford had plotted to do, regain custody of Laney for no reason other than to steal her inheritance. Norma had been unaware that Laney was an heiress and thought Anne would have mentioned it if it were true. Norma was, after all, the family lawyer.

Gin had raised more questions than answers, but one question Norma could answer. The property Laney was to inherit had to be the Samoset Way beach access, because her grandfather had owned it and it had value for Crawford. What she couldn't understand was why Gin and Crawford were hell-bent on getting their hands on Laney's land when Crawford, or at least Red River Resort, already owned it. But assuming there were a compelling reason, wouldn't Buddy Todd have been first in line to inherit from his father, and didn't that fact give Gin motive to kill Buddy Todd?

That Anne's daughter could plot and carry out a murder took some getting used to. Was she also the one who killed Crawford? Her grief over his death had seemed genuine. Norma struggled to believe Gin was not only capable of drowning Buddy Todd, but skillful enough to outsmart Crawford into trusting her. Based on Norma's observations of the man, Crawford had been no one's fool.

It was possible the murders were unrelated. Crawford had probably made many enemies along the way. Norma resolved to keep that possibility open, but adhere to the over-arching theme guiding Coigne and her from the beginning: All mysteries relating to the corpse on the beach led to Laney.

Gin's hand shook as she reached for her Bloody Mary. The woman was fragile and nervous, but why? Maybe she was frightened that her mother knew she'd tried to steal Laney's inheritance. Norma seized that lever and pulled. "In answer to your question, Gin, your mother doesn't know about your attempted swindle. Not yet. But she will when I tell her."

"You. You wouldn't." Gin's voice trailed away as she looked over Norma's shoulder.

Norma turned around. The waiter was coming back with their food. "Put that down and get out of here, you condescending pimp!" The waiter looked too startled to do anything but exactly as told. "That'll teach him," Norma said to herself, remembering the haughty look on his face.

Norma got back to business. "I have no need to tell your mother of your criminal activities if I get what I want, Gin. If I don't, my telling your mother will be the least of your worries."

"That's blackmail."

"That's right. What, you think you're the only one capable of familial felony?" Norma had just made up the legal term, but liked the sound of it. All those Fs and Ls sounded like a minimum twenty years in the pokey. "The first thing you're going to do is march down to the State Police Barracks in Skaket and help identify the man who came to the breakfast table yesterday and spoke to Ken Crawford. He may be the one who kidnapped Laney, not that you've expressed the least bit of concern. Then, I want every piece of paper, gift, recording, anything and everything you ever received from Ken Crawford. If you leave anything out, I'll finger you for Buddy's and Crawford's murder. And Lieutenant Coigne will believe me. So will the jury."

Gin deposited several sugar packets into her purse and stood to go. "That's ridiculous. I would never have hurt Kenny."

"Your omission suggests to me you would have hurt Buddy."

"Go to hell."

24

Coigne replaced the phone, leaned back, and propped his feet on his desk. He closed his eyes and pressed his fingers against his temples. He'd just finished a call with Norma in which he'd heard all about her interview with Gin Sager. The call left him feeling the way any exposure to Norma did, no matter how brief, no matter the topic. He wanted to bang his head against the wall and, at the same time, drag her off to a cave for a week of sex.

What was it about that woman? Anyone else would keep his distance. She was unreasonable and at times downright cruel. Yet he found himself bewitched. He knew how a hunter felt when hot on the trail of a lethal animal. He wanted to be the one to drop the net, but was scared as hell to get too close.

As for the looks department, Norma was magnificent. He could easily imagine her donning a long white gown and raising her arms before a crowd of millions, holding them in her thrall. What you saw when you looked her in the eye was bold, stark intelligence—not the dull, wordy kind, the penetrating, arousing kind.

He shook his head in bafflement. He couldn't explain the attraction. He just knew he felt it and had to be careful or he'd find his manhood chopped to pieces.

He was wondering if he should have brought her fully into the investigation, shared with her what he knew about Sandal Man and she didn't. On the one hand, telling her could bring them closer to solving the case and finding Laney, if she was still alive, poor kid. Norma might just make something out of the information he'd uncovered, whereas his own brain was mired in possibilities, but no solutions. On the other hand, for all her smarts and experience in law, Norma was still a civilian. It wasn't prohibited to involve her fully in the investigation if he judged her helpful and not harmful to it. But he didn't know her well enough to make that assessment. If wrong he could lose his job or, much worse, lose Laney Sager.

He had to admit she'd handled the interview with Gin well. The tip about Laney's inheritance might explain Sandal Man's motive in kidnapping her, if that's what happened.

The phone rang.

"Coigne," he snapped, irritated at having his woolgathering disturbed. As the caller went on, Coigne let his feet drop to the floor. "Hold on. You're going too fast." He opened his desk drawer and reached for a pen and pad. "Give me that again." He kept writing, his face taut. "How'd you get all this?"

More talking.

"I'll be there in ten."

He shouted down the hall, "Be back."

"Hey, where are you going?" someone called.

The stairwell at the Barracks was steep, but bounding downward, Coigne was already pushing through the door when the question penetrated his brain. "Out."

Without giving his inner debate about Norma another thought, he called her from his cruiser, filled her in, and said he'd pick her up at her place. Before she could barrage him with questions, he hung up. He had mentally tossed his qualms out the window. There was no one on the force he could count on to make this case a priority in the way Norma would. He grabbed the debris in the passenger seat and threw it in the backseat.

Norma got in. "You look like shit, Coigne." She refused to strap on her seat belt, so it was over the ding-ding-ding sound that she said, "Give me the details, word for word. What did they find, and how, for God's sake?"

"Call came in fifteen minutes ago." He waited for the final ding. "You know we've brought in help from Cockle Cove and Skaket to help in the search. Young trooper named Katepoo—

don't look at me like that. His family's from Asia—Jimmy Katepoo called. He's young, but sharp and aggressive with his cases, lives in Skaket. He was out on his bike this morning, not even on duty today but looking for the girl near Marymac Pond. Was crossing Route 136 and his damn bike runs over a sandal, nearly throws him."

Norma didn't miss a beat. "Jade beads on the big toe ring?"

"You got it. Someone's taking it to Anne Sager for identification right now, but it certainly matches the size and description she gave us."

"Any signs of . . ."

Coigne never thought he'd hear Norma's voice quaver. His own softened. "No violence. No evidence of it at that location."

They rode the rest of the way in silence except that Norma fiddled incessantly with the air conditioner vents, cursing under her breath.

They came to a police barricade and, after Coigne said a few words to a young officer, they were ushered through. He introduced Norma to Trooper Katepoo, who led them to the spot on the pavement where the sandal was found. Katepoo had a high forehead, the only feature that kept him from being standard issue handsome, but his cheerful manner helped him out. Police were still combing the roadside for other evidence that Laney had been there, but according to Katepoo, nothing had turned up.

"We're hoping she dropped her sandal on purpose," he said to Coigne.

Norma asked why, although she thought she knew.

"It would show she was conscious and might be able to drop other clues."

Coigne said, "Do you agree she dropped the shoe after the swim in the pond? Kind of surprising she still had it after that."

"I do, sir. The pond's right off the bike path, where she started out. We're almost four miles due north of there."

Coigne looked at Norma for input. She was staring into the distance, seemingly dazed, and he wondered if she might be caving in to the strain after all. He left her a moment to question another trooper about the scope of the roadside search. They made plans to call in Air Wing assistance. He knew he'd meet with resistance from dispatch and the unit commander if he authorized the helicopter himself, but there wasn't time to go up the chain of command. He figured he'd be on solid ground if later challenged. He also instructed the trooper to contact neighbors for a line-walk of the area. When he looked back again, Norma had vanished.

25

Anne confirmed for one of the Tarleton Twins, as Norma had called them, it was Laney's sandal found on Route 136. The officer jotted the information in his pad and was preparing to leave when Gin arrived. Her long-simmering anger at her mother had been stoked to full conflagration during breakfast with Norma and she revived the flames with an attack against Anne for failing to protect Laney. The charge of negligent supervision was well-trodden ground between the women. Their raging battle allowed the officer to slip out, but without an audience their argument soon lost heat.

Anne left the living room to lie down and returned a half-hour later ready to call a truce. "You want something to eat? We need to keep up our strength."

"No. I'm getting a drink."

"God, Gin. Can you just stop?" Anne gave up. An argument required energy and she'd run out.

Standing in the center of the room, unsure what to do next, she stared at a strand of Laney's hair on the floor, caught by a stream of sunlight. She bent to pick it up. "Now how does it go? I won't let them harm a hair on your head?" She tried to shut out the clatter in the kitchen where Gin was making her drink and wandered over to the piano. She ran her hand along its sleek ebony casing, a habit before starting to play. Gordon always said the gesture made him think of a young girl patting the flank of her beloved black stallion. She sat down and without conscious thought began playing a Brahms sonata. It was one Laney liked.

Anne put her heart into the dynamics of the piece, hoping that if she played the notes just right, her precious granddaughter would hear and follow them home.

Gin slammed a door upstairs and caused Anne to lose concentration. She pulled the cover down over the keys. If she did not occupy her mind, she'd go mad. She considered sleeping pills or other anesthetics so she could stop thinking, but she could never do such a thing while Laney was still—what? Away? Yes, that was a safe word. While Laney was away.

In addition to playing piano, Anne often controlled anxiety by organizing things, her jewelry box or chest of drawers or music collection. She thought now of the most daunting of messes requiring a clean-out and her large, cluttered cloak room came to mind.

She surveyed the litter of stray boots, gloves, drum sticks, tennis rackets and vacuum parts. Beneath it all was the same wide-planked pine flooring that ran through the rest of the cottage, only some prior owner, an artist, had painted this floor white with large black diamonds. The diamonds were pretty well worn away by years of families and guests dropping things off or burrowing through the wide coat rack for the light-blue windbreaker or the full-length parka.

Overwhelmed with fatigue, she was unsure whether or not to take on the task and turned back toward the cloakroom entrance. Laney's backpack hung on a hook and Anne realized it had been there since the discovery of the beach murder. She loosened the tie and poured the contents onto the floor. Amidst the sunscreen, sunglasses, book, and sand, one item seemed out of place, an empty pack of cigarettes. *Like mother, like daughter?* Anne held the pack in her hand. "Gold Flake." She'd never seen the brand before, not that she'd ever smoked. She considered asking Gin about it, but the sting from her daughter's likely retort sent her instead to the Internet. It was a way to keep busy.

Gold Flake came up immediately and, as she scrolled through other ads about the brand, she saw that it was a popular one in India. She reached for it to look more closely, then snapped her hand back, as if she'd burned it.

She tried to reassure herself. "Probably nothing." Laney had done what she'd seen her Gran do for years, pick up someone else's garbage with the intention of throwing it away. Anne refused to panic over the cigarette pack, but immediately gave Lieutenant Coigne a call.

26

Norma thought about the sandal and how it had dropped or been tossed miles from where Laney's bike was found next to Marymac Pond. Obviously a car was used in her kidnapping. She couldn't imagine anyone hauling a struggling, 110 pound girl that distance, even through the woods.

The police were focusing their evidence-gathering on the road itself, having set up barricades, crime tape, and detour signs in the vicinity of where the sandal had been found. They hadn't yet explored the field of tall grasses on the west side of the road. Norma scanned it carefully, noting that not a blade of grass was bent much less broken. She turned to the east, where the road was bordered by woods. Nothing would be gained by standing around and watching the police. She plunged into the teeming pines, unsure which way to go or what she was even looking for. About a half mile in, she stopped. Why not get a map, figure out where the woods led and who owned the woods? As it was, she may as well have been searching blindfolded. She decided to forge ahead awhile longer and her perseverance paid off. She stumbled onto a gravel road and followed the tire tracks. *Road must lead to something,* she thought. *Probably some family has a cottage back there. With my luck they'll call the police on me for trespassing.*

The thought of police brought Coigne to mind. She'd been shoulder to shoulder with him for more than two days now, on the lookout for signs he was what his reputation said he was, rotten. On the contrary, he treated her well and solicited her advice.

But the more she dwelled on his apparent kindness, the louder her inner warning became. Out of nowhere she remembered playing in the backyard with her younger brother, Mike. It was a sticky, buggy summer afternoon and they hadn't eaten all day. Their father was out of work and looking after them while their mother took a few months off, as she was wont to do. "Looking after them" consisted of telling them to go play in the backyard while he watched TV.

She and Mike played airplane, taking turns flying off the back steps, each time ascending one step higher for take-off. On the final take-off, Norma crashed and cut her head open. The bleeding soaked her shirt and formed a red bib across her chest. Mike ran for their father, who rushed out. "God!" he said. He gently tilted her chin upward so he could examine the wound. He'd never used such a light touch on her before. His kindness was unexpected and for a moment she felt loved. Then he slapped her face so hard she fell down again. "I said play in the back*yard*, not on the steps." She didn't like to think of her childhood, but knew such warning memories were for her own good.

Her pace slowed as the dense heat in the middle of the woods made breathing tough. The sweat beneath her waist band irritated her. She'd left her hat in Coigne's cruiser and her shoulder-length hair felt like plaited mail on her shoulders. "I suppose a guy can be sensitive to the needs and feelings of others while cheating the hell out of the public for his own benefit." Yet she didn't know of any such person. Even while her mind sifted through several layers of painful worries, the possible whereabouts of Laney, the lawsuit pending against her, the imminent burst of blisters on her heels, she continued thinking about Coigne. Maybe he was only dirty when his "victim" was a bad guy. *Was that so wrong? Yes. For one thing, maybe the bad guy victim wasn't a bad guy after all. For another, it was dishonest and if you're willing to screw one guy, it's a lot easier to screw the next, and so on and so forth.* By then she'd walked another mile and found herself standing beneath a canopy of leafy branches. She looked ahead. "Bingo."

The cottage, although surrounded by bird calls and squirrel skitterings, was not peaceful. It was devoid of the usual Cape cuteness: café curtains, window boxes filled with pansies, and brightly painted shutters. Raccoon scat and wasp nests littered the front porch. Torn lace curtains looked like spider webs. It was hopeless trying to see through the window panes on the locked front door. She knew if she broke in she could get into trouble for trespassing and possibly destroying evidence at a crime scene, but instinct told her something was wrong and she needed to get inside. She removed her blouse and, wrapping it around her fist, shattered a pane. Sticking her arm through and unlocking the door, she went in, with a final word to the squirrels. "You want to sue me? Get in line."

"You in there, Norma?" Coigne's voice called from outside.

Norma left the kitchen to find Coigne and Trooper Katepoo standing side by side in the front hall. She said, "Took you long enough. Laney was here." She held up what looked like a colorful worm. It was an anklet of braided string. She dropped it in Coigne's outstretched hand saying, "Clever girl, huh?"

"You sure it's hers?"

"Of course I'm sure. The sandal. The anklet. She may be scared, Coigne, but not enough to keep her from helping us find her." She turned away, surprised by the stinging in her eyes. "And go see the bathroom, if you can stand the stink. There's a small bar of soap and it's still moist. Tell me I'm seeing things, but I think there's an L etched in it."

"Don't touch anything else, Norma." Coigne pulled out his cell phone and nodded to his trooper and then toward the living room. Trooper Katepoo guided Norma by her elbow like she was mother-of-the-bride being seated in her pew.

When he'd finished his call, Coigne looked around the cottage and then joined them in the living room.

"I don't think they hurt her. Do you, Coigne?"

Coigne gazed at Norma for what seemed like a long time, which frightened her. Then he said, "I don't see evidence of it."

Soon the cottage was overtaken by Crime Scene Services. They were like a pack of beagles nosing around foxholes. Norma went outside, promising to sit on the edge of the drive and not move. She wasn't going to leave if forensics might make other discoveries. After a while, her legs cramped from sitting cross-legged and she stood. Laney had been in the cottage. *Okay, so then what? Had she been out on the road where she lost a sandal, gotten picked up and taken to the cottage? Or was she taken to the cottage first and somehow escaped to the road, where she was trapped again? Where are you, Laney?*

It was almost sundown by the time Coigne dropped Norma back at her house. She closed the cruiser door, but paused at the open passenger window. "You let me know if they find anything immediately, Coigne. I want to hear from you first thing in the morning."

Coigne rolled his eyes. "Yes, Boss." He started to leave, then stopped, his face turning serious. "You'll hear from me as appropriate."

Norma frowned. "Why the Dragnet voice? We have a deal. I'm telling you everything I know, you're telling me everything you know. Right?"

"That's not a *deal*, Norma. You're telling me everything you know because you don't want to pervert the course of justice."

"Don't give me that Criminal Procedure 101 crap. What are you trying to say?"

Coigne picked at an invisible splinter on his thumb. "You've been a big help today, Norma. We wouldn't have found the cottage for some time without you." He put the cruiser in gear. "I'll call you."

Coigne's sudden frostiness worried Norma. *Wasn't she part of the investigative team? Hell, she'd practically led the investigative team.*

As Coigne drove off, she shared with him something she'd learned from her French lover, "Pole." She gave him the full *bras d'honneur*.

27

Norma shook off Coigne's odd behavior and made her way down the brick path to her front door. Memories of the night Bark died caused her to take a half-crouched position as she stepped inside. It was dusk and everything looked shadowy and vague. She saw no boogey man perched on the stairs and her files were stacked as she'd left them. Still, she felt the heaviness of a presence and it filled her with unease. All too soon, the source made himself known.

"Oh good. I was afraid you'd be gone all night, out with the police on some errand of derring-do. Join me for a drink?" Derek Dohnan toasted her with a glass of her own scotch. He sat tucked in a leather armchair by the fireplace, stomach protruding over splayed legs, lord of the manor.

"How did you get in here?"

"I guess you could say turnabout is fair play, Norma."

His tone was cheerful. He reminded her of a fat cat. She could almost see canary feathers sticking to his greasy mug.

"You're right about one thing, Dohnan. I have been working with the police. In fact, one of them just dropped me off and should be able to turn back and arrest you, P-D-Q." She started to leave to get her phone.

"And I'll say you invited me in to discuss the Cockle Cove-Temple litigation." In a sing-song voice he added, "Phone records will show we spoke this morning." He gave the arm of his chair a swift pat.

As a general rule Norma wouldn't hesitate to go on fighting and even call Coigne back, but this time she was more curious to know why Dohnan had broken in. "What do you want?"

"All in good time, Norma. Fix me another drink, will you?" He held up his glass, which she ignored. "Or better yet, come sit by me. No reason we can't be friends. I've always been fond of you."

"I'll get you the drink."

When she returned, Norma was reminded about that time at The Lucky Duck, how Dohnan would pull at an imaginary goatee every time he lobbed a whopping lie. He was at it again.

"Get on with it, Dohnan. I'm very tired and you're very ugly." She handed him the scotch.

"Ha!" His voice now lowered a notch, from wheedling to intimate. "Please, Norma. Have a seat. I suspect there's something you want to ask me, something you've perhaps discovered in your review of my files?"

Norma had indeed something to ask Dohnan. He'd been the lawyer for Old Man Todd. Now he was representing the Temple brothers in a suit against her. Something was wrong with that picture. Norma mentally reviewed the professional conduct rules for a Massachusetts attorney. It wasn't a conflict of interest for Dohnan to represent Old Man Todd in his land sale, then represent the Temple brothers to recover their Red River Resort interest and indirectly recover the same piece of land. It would be a problem if he'd tried to represent the Temple brothers against Old Man Todd, to recover the land. No, the problem had to be elsewhere.

She went back to basics. Dohnan was a swindler. Since he was now hell bent on getting big dollars into the hands of the Temple brothers, and presumably a kickback for himself, maybe he'd been working with them all along at the same time he'd represented Old Man Todd. Maybe he'd tricked Old Man Todd out of his land. But then why had Dohnan and the brothers allowed Mary Temple to sell to the resort? Had they really been surprised by the sale, as they now claimed? And why had Old Man Todd sold property that, according to Gin Sager, he'd intended for Laney to inherit? Her head ached.

"I'm sorry, Norma. Did you say something?"

"You attached to your draft Complaint an agreement between Mary Temple and her sons that contained language giving the Temple brothers a right of first refusal in Mary's Red River Resort interest. That version of the agreement was not in existence at the time of the sale."

"You are incorrect. The copy I attached to the Complaint was notarized at the time of the execution by the Temple brothers and their mother, and that was at the time of the sale."

"Then your clients' beef is not with me but with their mother, and now her estate. But of course it would be silly to pursue her estate, as they are her heirs and their suit would only deplete the size of their inheritance. So, they're after me. And by the way, who drafted that agreement between Mary Temple and her sons?"

"I did, of course."

"That's interesting. I didn't see that agreement in your files."

"But unfortunately that's not a claim you can make in your defense, is it, or you'd have to admit how you came to have access to my files."

Speaking of files, how did she know Dohnan wasn't the one who'd knocked her out, ransacked her files, trashed her home and killed Bark? Did he look the type, smooth skin, porcine snout? He was certainly creepy enough, but not like a thug, more like a pedophile. If he was responsible, he'd hired someone to do the dirty deeds. She'd find out, but first she'd try to get some easy answers.

"How is it that you come to be representing the Temple brothers?"

"Let's face it, Norma. You were hired by Mary Temple, a kindly, unsophisticated widow, because you had helped her with her—what was it—the Hospital Auxiliary or something. After she died, her sons wanted to hire someone with clout, someone who knows his way around, someone used to playing with the big boys. You're on your own. You work from home—no infrastructure, no bench, deep or otherwise. Not exactly a confidence-inspiring set-up."

"The future of American jurisprudence isn't exactly in the hands of Dunscomb and Dohnan."

He expanded on her other professional inadequacies, but she paid no attention, her mind focused on whether he had other "proof" of an error on her part, beyond the agreement he'd attached to the Complaint. She was certain she'd asked Mary whether there was anything that would prevent her from selling her interest to her Red River partners. There were attestations in her file signed by Mary to the effect that there were none. Still, Dohnan probably had enough with that agreement to keep Norma tied up in knots for some time. The dated signatures on his agreement looked legitimate and his copy was notarized. So what did he want with her this evening?

Dohnan bent over the side of his chair. Only then did Norma notice his brief-case. He lifted it onto his lap and flipped open the brass tabs with his thumbs. He drew out a document and handed it to her. "A compromise is the only way out, Norma. I know your financial status." He looked pointedly around the room. "You can't afford to defend the lawsuit, much less pay damages.

She glanced through the pages. "What is this crap?"

"The document should be familiar to you. It's a settlement agreement you signed in a suit with facts similar to the one the Temple brothers are going to file against you. They're almost identical. You overlooked three consents needed for a sale transaction ten years ago and the oversight cost your client plenty."

"That's baloney. My insurance company insisted on a nuisance value settlement from me. That claim against me was as bogus as yours."

"Nevertheless, it won't look good for you in a second malpractice suit."

"You won't get that admitted, dummy."

"I might. Besides, we're not asking you for much. We're simply asking you not to contradict us if you're called as a witness against Red River Resort for swindling Mrs. Temple out of her partnership interest. In return, we won't sue you for overlooking the right of first refusal provision."

"Of course they didn't swindle her out of her interest. You're asking me to lie under oath. This sounds like extortion and suborning perjury. Am I on the right track?"

"That's the idea.

"Don't worry. We probably won't get to trial. We aim to squeeze Red River Resort right up to the moment of their zoning board hearing. You have no doubt heard they're working on a sizeable development. My hunch is they'll be only too happy to settle quite handsomely with us to avoid litigation and a scandal at this sensitive time."

Despite her revulsion, she forced herself to think through Dohnan's proposition. A decision tree appeared in her mind and she followed each branch to its end. The possibility of getting out of the lawsuit would tempt anyone. She made up her mind and stretched out her hand for a shake.

Dohnan stood up and grabbed at his invisible goatee. "Norma, your worries are over."

"Get out."

28

Norma slept only two hours and those were fitful. The Dohnan experience the night before had left her addled. She needed something painfully aerobic, like a quick run, to restore her mental faculties, but a phone call from Anne made her change plans. Her friend seemed out of breath with excitement. Coigne still had no word on Laney's whereabouts but had good reason to believe she was alive. He wanted them to meet him at the Barracks at 11:00 to review the forensic results from the cottage.

Hearing the relief in Anne's voice, Norma felt ashamed she hadn't been the one to contact Anne the night before about Laney's sandal and the other discoveries made at the cottage. She could have let Anne know Laney was probably alive. Coigne had beaten her to it.

As she hung up the phone, Norma wondered if Gin was also invited to the 11:00 meeting. Anne hadn't said anything about her, but whether that meant Gin wasn't in shape to go or Anne hadn't told her about the meeting, Norma didn't know.

The women agreed to meet at the park, in the center of Cockle Cove, since Norma wanted to stop by the tax assessor's office to find out who owned the cottage where Laney had been held. She knew Coigne would have this information when they arrived and it was foolish of her to spend time duplicating his efforts, but she felt it was important to show she had the information too. Coigne needed to see her as an essential ally or he wouldn't keep her in the loop.

The tax clerk was intelligent and willing to help. The owner of the cottage turned out to be a straw party, which didn't surprise Norma nor did it help, but she was willing to bet her right arm Sandal Man was behind that straw party. She noted the tax clerk's name as she said good-bye on her way out. Another Katepoo. Astounding. And how convenient for Coigne to have a trooper's relative in a government office. An idea struck her and she made a mental note to follow up when she could.

Norma arrived at the park early and took a moment to catch her breath, scanning the block in case Anne showed up early, too. The flower boxes bordering Main Street were overflowing with pink, purple, and white petunias. The park had been turned into a sea filled with colorful sharks, dozens of them. The display was prompted by recent tourist-titillating shark sightings. The local dentist sponsored a shark with sparkling white teeth and the jeweler's sported a diamond-studded tail. Norma had never seen a shark display sponsored by a big law firm—maybe a little redundant.

Down the street she spotted Anne wedging her Prius behind an SUV the size of an M1 Abrams. Norma challenged herself to list as many of the family transport tank models as she could think of—Durango, Sequoia, Wrangler, Renegade, Yukon, and Tundra. The names sweated with brute force and true grit, traits essential for surviving the journey through a quaint village like Cockle Cove.

From a distance she could tell Anne had been crying. Her eyes were swollen with worry. Norma ignored the nearby crosswalk and darted through horn-blaring traffic, halting it to retrieve her fishing hat. Without a word she embraced her friend. Norma knew that with her skinny arms there was no way she could execute a comforting hug, but she got her friend to crack a weak smile.

"I don't know what's the matter with me, Norma. I've kept myself together for days and now there's actually some hope, I'm falling apart."

"The fact that you're coping at all is miraculous. You're doing great. Quit blubbering and let's go."

They took Norma's car and arrived at the Barracks one minute before 11:00. While they waited, Norma asked if Gin was to meet with Coigne, too.

"She's been MIA since yesterday afternoon. Said she was heading back to her room at Red River Resort to pack, but I haven't been able to reach her."

A young woman escorted them to an office where Coigne was finishing a phone call. Norma sat down and thought about the fact that Coigne had contacted Anne instead of her about this meeting. It was a clear sign of a guilty conscience because he'd been holding out on her last night, but about what? Confronting him head on might antagonize him and wouldn't lead to an answer. Besides, it was a new day. Let bygones be bygones. She'd be on her best behavior.

Coigne hung up the phone and tilted his styrofoam cup side-to-side. "Coffee, ladies?"

"We're not here for chitchat, Coigne. You have forensic test results? What are they?"

"Norma." Anne placed a hand on her friend's arm.

"Sorry." So much for self-restraint.

"Let's get started then." Coigne explained that he'd just been on the phone with Trooper Katepoo, who joined them at that instant.

"I think you've met Norma Bergen. Anne Sager, this is Trooper James Katepoo."

Anne reached up to shake his hand but Norma jumped in. "What have you got, Katepoo?"

He glanced at Coigne. "We've been able to reconstruct the girl's—Laney's—movements in the cottage. It's obvious she was held for some time in the kitchen pantry. That's where you found the ankle bracelet, Ms. Bergen."

"I know that."

"Latent prints, hair strands, and possibly the letter L in the bathroom soap suggest she was in the bathroom and also sat for some time in an armchair in the living room, maybe talking to someone. We're still waiting for confirmation from AFIS."

"Explain that, Trooper Katepoo."

"Yes, sir. It's the Automated Fingerprint Identification System. That's a federal computer system that stores fingerprints in a searchable database." He paused. A slight lift of the shoulder from Coigne gave him the go-ahead to continue. "We can't be certain, but based on bits of blood in the front hall and porch floor boards and the impressions in the driveway, she was knocked about in the front room and took a fall, or was pushed, down the stairs."

Anne shut her eyes. Norma reached over and squeezed her hand.

"There wasn't significant blood loss, Ms. Sager, and it's clear she got up and walked, maybe was pushed, into the woods. Anyway, she was on her own two feet."

"So who was it? *Who* pushed her?" Norma tried to sound all business but it was hard.

"The guy may have been wearing gloves or wiped down the furniture, doorknobs, whatever, there weren't any prints." Then something made Jimmy Katepoo smile. "Amazing thing. We found a switchblade at the entry point to the woods. Must have fallen out of someone's pocket. It was covered in beautiful fingerprints. We matched them with a local thug's. He hangs out in Skaket, name of Lancelot Varn."

"Lancelot? Are you kidding me?"

"No, Ms. Bergen."

"That was a rhetorical question, Katepoo." Norma turned to Coigne. "Did you pick him up?"

"Even if we knew where he was," Coigne said, "we wouldn't have picked him up yet. He's just muscle. He isn't smart enough, obviously—consider his leaving that knife behind—to have masterminded the grab."

The women digested the information. Then, with a growing sense she was right Norma said, "You know who the mastermind is."

Coigne didn't answer at first. He shuffled through his notes as if preparing to say something about their contents. He turned toward Anne. "Lancelot Varn has recently been associated with a Rahul Singh, a business mogul originally from Mumbai."

"Mumbai," Anne repeated, her voice not more than a whisper. She sank back in her chair.

"So what's his shtick?" Norma looked from Coigne to Katepoo and back to Coigne.

"Singh is into drugs, money laundering, insider trading, human trafficking—you name it," Coigne said.

"He diversifies," Katepoo threw in, but his quip didn't get a chuckle. He cleared his throat.

"Singh's known to the FBI for racketeering," Coigne went on, "and we've had an eye on him because of some real estate deals on the Cape."

"Human trafficking," Anne said.

Norma thought fast. The only thing she knew about human trafficking was the phone number to call if you suspected it, which was posted on websites and doors of ladies' room stalls.

"Don't jump to conclusions, Ms. Sager. We're not even sure it's Rahul Singh."

"But of course you are sure, Lieutenant."

Norma stared at Anne. Her friend's statement was made with such *sang-froid*. Where was that coming from? Even the thought of Laney in the hands of such a monster as this Singh turned Norma's stomach. Yet here was Anne, certain that this guy from the underworld was Rahul Singh. She acted as though she'd heard of him.

Anne answered Norma's unvoiced question when she said to Coigne, "You're sure it's Singh because I gave you a cigarette pack from Laney's backpack. It's from India, isn't it? I looked it up on the Internet."

"What cigarette pack? What's she talking about, Coigne? Why don't I know about this?" Coigne's only answer was a steady, annoying clicking of his pen. Trooper Katepoo remained mute, eyes fixed on the floor.

"I think I know what happened," Anne said. "Rahul Singh killed the man on the beach, Laney's father—I say father, but his paternity claims, that's another issue." Anne looked disgusted, but quickly got back on track. "Singh, or maybe it was this Lancelot character, was foolish enough to leave evidence behind—a cigarette pack. Not just any pack, but an unusual one imported from India. Singh realized Laney must have picked it up. She'd seen him return for his sandals when they first met. Laney said as much to you on the day you interviewed her, Lieutenant. To get the cigarette pack back, Singh had to find out where it was, so he had her kidnapped. Do I have it right?"

"That's certainly one theory, Ms. Sager." Shifting in his chair, Coigne launched into a lecture titled "The Risks of Jumping to Conclusions," but still his ball-point clicked away.

Anne's hands were balled into tight fists. "But what other explanation could there be?"

"Okay Ms. Sager, you may be right, but if so, if that's the only reason he kidnapped her, once she told him where the pack was he would have...he would have had no further use for her. Your house would have been broken into, the pack retrieved, and that would have been that."

To Norma, Coigne sounded nervous, but not about the motive for Laney's kidnapping. It was something else. Norma was sure of it. "Stop clicking that damn pen, Coigne."

Coigne put the pen down and let Anne continue to theorize, but Norma wasn't listening anymore. The pieces were slowly fitting together. Coigne had been evasive with her the night before because he already knew about Singh. Anne had given him the cigarette pack, she'd said. That gave him a clue, which must have tied into other suspicions he had.

"Why didn't you tell me about the cigarette pack sooner, Coigne? And about Singh? You've known about him awhile." Norma's voice was quiet, but its menace roared.

"Trooper, would you take Ms. Sager for coffee while Norma and I discuss—"

"I don't care if they hear this, Coigne. Anne, you should know that Coigne has been sitting on this information and if I'd had it sooner we might be closer to getting Laney back." Norma felt a twinge because she'd sat on information about the cottage Anne would have found helpful too. But the insight was fleeting.

"Now wait a minute." Coigne stood as Katepoo steered Anne out of the room.

From the door Anne said, "You should have told her everything, Lieutenant."

Norma got up, too. "What they say about you must be true, Coigne. You can't be trusted. You act like you're playing fair, but you're not. You used me to get as much information as you could, but you held out on me. You probably kept Singh's identity to yourself for ego reasons, so you could get all the credit if—*when* Laney is found."

"That's enough, Norma," Coigne said, hands on his hips.

"Singh isn't even a dangerous criminal to you. He's probably a-a revenue source."

"You should leave right now."

29

Laney wasn't sure where Mr. Singh had brought her, but she'd been sitting in the dark for hours smelling fish. The powerful odor reminded her of the summer Gran first showed her the East Nauset Fish Pier. They'd stood on a walkway overlooking Jeremy's Cove. Gran had stooped to Laney's eye level and pointed toward Moonlight Bay, then steered her arm around like a mounted telescope toward Scrub Island, over to Cranberry Beach, and then to the break at the entrance to Nauset Harbor. Is that where she was now, the East Nauset Fish Pier?

"Not in the face, Varn. She might have salvage value."

She thought hard about the question of where she was, to avoid seeing Varn's fist raised, and tried not to cry as Mr. Singh left the room. She would keep thinking of that day with her Gran.

"Get up. I said *get up*. You think you can make me look like a *fool* by escaping like that? No one makes me look like a *fool*. I'll show you who's the *fool*." Varn punctuated each sentence with a punch to her stomach until she sank to her knees.

Gran had remarked on the clunk of heavy chains as dark, tattooed men in waders loaded aqua-colored crates into stacks. The men smoked cigarettes and called to one another, but their words were drowned out by the screech of seagulls.

Varn gave his fist a rest and started kicking her. "Where is it? Where is the letter?"

In her mind the high tide and a gleeful swarm of seagulls had led the fishing boats home with their catch. She'd stood mesmerized as their holds emptied onto a steel slide that disappeared beneath the walkway. Thousands of squirming, bloody dogfish flipped about and cascaded down the slide. Just when she thought the show was over, a baby dogfish, on its own, slithered down after them.

With one swift kick to her head Varn said, "Don't worry. Where you're going, brain damage is a good thing."

Laney had asked Gran what became of the fish at the end of the slide. "Those stacked lockers are headed around the world. The spiny dogfish go to England for fish and chips, Germany for shillerlocken, and China for soup."

Laney passed out.

Thirty minutes later Laney awakened to a shaft of light pouring through a dirty window up near the ceiling. She made out low voices and heard Varn say, "What if she doesn't know?" and Mr. Singh snap back, "Of course she knows. Why was her father frequenting her neighborhood if not to give her the letter?"

Their voices faded in and out. Laney would have laughed at the endless questions about a letter if she hadn't been sure it would hurt too much. She tried once more to explain that she didn't know her father, so how could she know about a letter he supposedly gave her, but no sound came out of her mouth. She blacked out again.

The next voice she heard was the last one she would have expected. It had to be a dream. But that voice, full of smoker's phlegm, was unmistakable. "Baby, wake up. You've got to tell them where your father's letter is."

"Mom?" Laney tried to sit up but couldn't, and fell back. She closed her eyes and tried not to think of what Varn meant by, "Where you're going, brain damage will be a blessing."

The dream persisted. When Laney opened her eyes, Varn had disappeared and Mr. Singh was in his place. Her mom was squatting beside her, her high heel sandals an inch deep in the dirt floor. "You poor baby," she whispered.

What was her mom doing here? Did she know these people? Was she here to rescue her? "Is Gran here too, Mom?"

Gin didn't answer, but stood and faced Mr. Singh. "So what's going on here, Rahul? She's been knocked out. Has that ape been hurting her?"

"We brought you here to get her to talk," Mr. Singh said. "Out of kindness, Gin. We do you a favor, you do us a favor. Do what it takes. I'll leave it to you." Mr. Singh headed to the door, but turned around. "Or we start on you."

The door closed and Gin crouched down beside Laney again. She reached for her daughter's shoulder and shook frantically. "You've got to wake up, Laney."

"That hurts!"

Gin placed her mouth near Laney's ear. "This is our big chance, baby."

"Mom, how do you know Mr. Singh?"

"I've been helping him, honey. Or really, he's been helping me. You know Kenny. Well, he and I were going to get ahold of that letter to your father and Kenny could keep his property and I'd be rich, we'd be rich, but then Kenny found out I was also working with his partner, Rahul. I needed the cash. They got into a big fight. I think Rahul had him killed, baby. So we've got to tell him what he wants. If we do, we get lots of money. We can go far away and buy anything we want."

"I don't know anything, Mom." Laney wasn't sure those words had come out. She was having such trouble understanding what was happening.

"The letter, silly. You've got to tell them where you put the letter your father had from Old Man Todd. The old geezer was giving you this valuable land, but then somebody sold it out from under him. We need that letter, hon. We have to get rid of it."

Laney still couldn't comprehend. She wanted to sleep.

"You've got to know. You've just *got* to know. Do you realize they'll start beating me if you don't tell them? This is for you, Laney. For you!"

Mr. Singh returned to the room, Varn two steps behind, and shined a flashlight in Gin's eyes. "Well?" He had dispensed with courtesy and was in a hurry. "What do you have for us, Gin?"

"I know she'll come up with it, Rahul. She says she doesn't remember, but it's coming to her. I can tell. A mother can tell."

"Enough." Mr. Singh turned to Varn. "Deal with her."

Varn wasted no time. He grabbed Gin's arm, bent it at the elbow and twisted it behind her back, lifting until she screamed.

Laney shouted, "Wait!"

Varn wasn't to be distracted from his work. He took Gin's hand and tugged on a finger until she screamed again.

"Wait!" Laney struggled to get up.

Varn didn't stop until Gin slumped to the floor in a heap. He rolled her over and pulled his belt out of his pants' loops.

Laney screamed, "I said wait!" She lunged for Varn's ankle to bite it.

"You want some, too?" Varn snapped the belt in Laney's direction.

Mr. Singh blocked Varn's arm, a slight courtesy returning to his voice. "Please, Varn, your impatience to do a thorough job may alarm our guests. Let's hear what our young lady has to say."

"I know where the letter is. I just didn't realize I knew until now. I didn't even understand that I had met my father before."

"Do not be concerned. We are not bothered by how you got there, just that you got there. Now, if you please, tell us where the letter is."

Laney knew better. Leverage. Aunt Norma used the word when she taught Laney to play Monopoly. "Know what your leverage is and never give it up." She knew she wasn't dealing with the Parker Brothers, but with two live criminals. She had to come up with something or they'd kill her mom. She was certain of it. "I'll lead you to the letter. You can't find it yourselves."

The harshness returned to Mr. Singh's voice. "Varn, if you please. Our young guest needs encouragement."

The belt was raised again. Laney knew what she had to do and she had to get it right. Her expression, her tone, it all had to be right. She had also learned from Aunt Norma that the only way to bluff successfully was not to bluff at all. You had to mean what you said.

She thought about her life, living with Gran and her new friendship with the most popular girl in her grade. She didn't want to die. But she had to say she was willing to die and mean it. She imagined heaven and how it had been explained to her. Any death at Varn's hand would be a mere flash compared to eternity.

She could handle that. Did her face look like she meant it? She stared not at Varn, but at Mr. Singh. Did he see fear? The longer she stared at him, the less she feared him. Her hand reached for Varn's belt, not because she thought it would be given to her, but to show herself that her hand did not shake.

"Go ahead, Varn. But if you touch my mom or me again, I won't tell anyone where the letter is. We're as good as dead anyway. I'd rather keep the letter my secret if I'm going to die. Why give you the satisfaction?"

Laney could hardly believe her eyes, yet it was true. Just as she had changed, something had changed in Mr. Singh.

"Let's go." Mr. Singh headed for the door, then turned and shouted at Varn. "I said let's go, moron." Pointing at Gin he told Varn, "Get that bitch on her feet." He seethed when he turned to Laney. "When we get outside, you open your mouth, you make a sound of any kind, you are dead and we move on."

30

Norma knew slamming the office door was childish because she wasn't even disgusted with Coigne. It was herself she was furious with for trusting the bastard to play fair.

She and Anne drove in silence to Anne's Prius. Norma wanted to gnaw on something said at the meeting that had perplexed her, but now, mad as she was, she couldn't remember what it was. She hoped like hell it would come to her, because otherwise she'd hit a dead end.

"This is a dead end, Norma. You've turned too soon. It's just a new development here."

"That's just what I need, a new development to avoid a dead end." Norma turned the car around.

"Norma?"

"Yes."

"You need to know how grateful I am you're my friend. At least with you there's some hope we'll get her back." Anne's voice choked.

"Now look. We'll find her. I'm certain of it. Back there I was mad at Coigne, but he's committed to finding her too. Don't let my beating up on him worry you. That's how I process, you know? Letting off steam." Norma let the words sink in and pulled in behind Anne's car. "Where the hell is Gin, anyway? I hope her excuse for her absence is that she's busy doing the homework assignment I gave her."

Anne chuckled softly. "I hope so too, although she's never done a lick of homework in her life."

As Anne opened the car door Norma said, "Wait a sec. I've got to get into Gin's room at Red River Resort. Any ideas?"

"Why? What are you looking for?"

"I'm not sure. Gin was to share with me everything Crawford ever gave her—notes, gifts, etc."

"Naturally she hasn't followed through. Not even the kidnapping of her own daughter—"

"Don't start, Anne."

"You're right. You're right." Anne rifled through her purse for tissue and blew her nose. "I think I need to lie down. I haven't slept the three days she's been gone." She rummaged for her cell phone. "Anyway, I have an idea about how you can get into Gin's room." She explained her idea while she did a quick Internet search for a number and dialed. "I had quite a conversation with the resort front desk when I was looking for Laney in the ladies room the other day. They may remember me and that I was with Gin and Ken Crawford, especially since that was the day he was killed. Give me a second."

She was able to connect with the same hotel clerk and make arrangements for Norma to "come by and pick up a few things," as Gin would now be staying at home with her.

"Well, that doesn't say much for hotel staff security training. You could have been anyone."

"This is the Cape, Norma."

"I'll let you know if I find anything important."

"Just find Laney. Please."

Gin's hotel room was huge and in light of the Do Not Disturb sign on the outside doorknob, its condition was much as Norma had pictured. The bed was unmade and Gin's tropical colored shoes, bras and panties dotted the furniture like decorative accents. Room service trays littered every surface. Despite the fact the bathroom was the size of a garage, Gin's make-up, toothpaste, lotions, pills and hair products managed to make it feel cluttered and cramped.

Norma pawed through the debris. She didn't know what she was looking for, but she was working on the premise that just because Crawford was dead didn't mean Gin was no longer interested in snatching Laney's inheritance out from under her. If Gin was still keen, how she went about pursuing that inheritance could give clues to Laney's kidnapping. It was a long shot, but all she had.

Near the bedside telephone, amidst mermaid's toenails, tiny saltwater clam shells, and a half-full glass of wine, she found a note. "Fs Peer-E.N."

"Hm. Fish Pier-E.N. Wait a minute. East Nauset. East Nauset Fish Pier." The note could be old and meaningless, but something told her Gin hadn't jotted it down to get a jump on cheap dogfish.

She felt her adrenaline surge as she hit the elevator button five times. When she got outside she phoned Coigne. She still hated his guts, but didn't want to confront kidnappers without some back-up. "Coigne, don't say anything about earlier today. I think I know where Laney was taken."

"Fish Pier."

There was a long pause. "As a matter of fact, yes. How do *you* know, or is this something else you've been hiding?"

"Look. Before anything else, we need to get that misunderstanding straightened out. I learned about the Gold Flake pack last evening after I dropped you off and told you about it in my office this morning. And yes, I had a suspicion that Singh was involved in Laney's kidnapping because of something *you* said about Ken Crawford having foreign investment partners in the Red River Resort."

"Okay, okay—"

"Quiet 'til I'm finished. I was able to get a list of partners and recognized one of Singh's old aliases. His photo was not inconsistent with Laney's description of Sandal Man. We've always felt that the Crawford murder was tied to Laney's disappearance. But how I arrived at these theories and suspicions is irrelevant. Norma, you are not a state trooper, even though you've been enormously helpful and I want your help to continue, but I have to maintain boundaries."

"You done?"

"Yes."

"I accept your apology. Now tell me how you know about the Fish Pier."

He sighed. "Fine. You know the supply shack down there. The owner fell asleep last night at the back of his shop. When he wakes up this morning he sees two guys by the water. Definitely not fishermen. He calls us. Anything suspicious, we're treating it like it may involve Laney. Trooper Katepoo went down to take a look right after our meeting this morning."

"Well, is she there?"

"No."

"So how do you know it wasn't some teenagers down there on a summer lark?" Of course she knew it wasn't, based on Gin's note, but she was hoping for a few more crumbs while he was in a talking mood.

"First of all, Red River Resort keeps a boat down at the pier, which we'd already searched early on but found nothing. Boat's still there by the way. But it means someone from the resort, like Singh, might be familiar with the pier. Second, we found blood, not much, in a storage room beneath the pier. Forensics is looking at hair strands that may be Laney's. So there's nothing definite yet, just working theories."

Norma thought, why bring Laney to the pier if not to take her somewhere by boat? But the boat was still docked and Laney was gone. Did something spook them? She voiced the question.

"Beats me," Coigne said. "Maybe they saw the supply shack owner and took off. "

Norma filled him in on her search of Gin's hotel room and the note. She signed off saying, "I'll meet you at the pier."

On her way, she thought about Coigne's explanation and acknowledged he might not be as guilty of hoarding information as she'd thought, but that didn't explain why Anne had not called her right away about the cigarette pack. Was she being presumptuous to think she had first dibs on everyone's information? The more she thought it over, the more she realized to her horror she was placing her desire to be kept abreast of everything before Laney's need to be rescued. Yet she honestly believed she was in the best position to put all the pieces of the puzzle together and find Laney, if she had the benefit of everyone's information. It wasn't pride, but confidence. She wouldn't let anyone, Coigne, the governor, the POTUS, anyone, keep her from getting information.

Yellow crime-scene tape across the pier's parking lot entrance failed to slow Norma down. "He couldn't tell someone I was coming?" She waved to Trooper Katepoo and drove through the tape.

He ran after her and made her park and get out, apologizing but explaining, "I've got to get instructions from the Lieutenant." He pulled out his phone.

Under other circumstances, halyards clanging softly in the warm breeze might have had a soothing effect on Norma, but now they marked time ticking away. She grabbed his phone and said, "I just got off the phone with Lieutenant Coigne. He'll be mad as hell that you delayed me. Go get some footies for me from those forensics guys before I trample on something important." She returned his phone. "Go!" She shoved past him, hoping her threatened destruction of a crime scene would get him moving.

Treading carefully, with only the flashlight from her phone to guide her, she arrived at a small room. The door was open, but the doorway was cordoned off by yellow tape. The overwhelming smell of fish almost discouraged her from lingering until her attention was drawn to a narrow shaft of light that lasered down from a high window to the dirt floor. There, it encircled a shiny object, but how to reach it? "Oh hell." She ducked under the tape, tiptoed to the object, wrapped her fingers in a corner of her blouse, and pulled on a piece of silver the size of a match head. With gentle tugging, a two-inch silver shark was freed from its burial in the dirt.

She drew in her breath. "Gin's necklace." She'd seen Gin put it on after her unplanned shower. *Had Gin been here with Laney? Was it left here on purpose for us to find?* The twisted and broken eyehole gave her no clue. Norma carefully searched around the area with her phone flashlight. Other than a spider and what looked like mouse turds, she came up empty.

The shark charm had to be a deliberate plant. Laney had already shown her cleverness in leaving physical clues behind.

Those clues seemed to hold no secondary meaning, just to say "I was here." But if the shark simply confirmed that she and her mother had been held captive in that room, why take the necklace chain, unless the shark itself was the point? Immediately she saw the weakness in her logic. The chain might have been noticed by Rahul Singh if left with the shark. Still, she wanted to believe the shark was the clue because she had an idea what it might mean.

"I'm sorry, Ms. Bergen—"

"Katepoo. You found the footies. Hold onto them. Call your boss. Tell him to meet me at the park in Cockle Cove. Tell him I found something and to hurry." She showed him the shark as she brushed past him.

"But you can't remove evidence. Hey wait!"

"And for God's sake don't leave your post. Coigne'll kill you."

31

"It was a good guess, Norma." Coigne started his engine with Norma sulking in the passenger seat.

"Nothing's good about a guess that doesn't lead anywhere."

"Much as I sympathize, you couldn't be more wrong. We've eliminated the possibility that the shark charm was intended to direct us to her next location. So we consider other possibilities."

"It eliminates nothing of the sort. The sharks display was just one of a multitude of locations the shark charm might lead us to."

"Fine. So we've eliminated one location. Let's think of others."

Norma despised these glass-as-half-full types. Sometimes facts were ugly and you needed to face them head-on. Yet even in her crushing disappointment about not finding any sign of Laney at the park in downtown Cockle Cove, she knew Coigne was trying to encourage her. She appreciated it.

"Norma, I have a proposal. Let's do our thinking while we get something to eat. How about Captain's Quarters?"

"Are you out of your mind? How can you think about eating when Laney is still missing?"

"I'll tell you how." Coigne was executing a flawless three-point turn. "I'm an experienced cop, and I know we need to eat if we're in this search for the long haul. It's been three days and these guys holding Laney are getting sloppy, and that's good. And by the way, no one said you have to eat. Just sit there while *I* figure out the most efficient deployment of my scarce resources so *I* can eliminate a few more of the multitude of locations. Okay?"

"All right. What's with the attitude?"

As they pulled into the Captain's Quarters parking lot, Coigne explained the tavern was family-owned, and, like its owners, unassuming. It was so unassuming it had no exterior signage to announce it was anything other than what it looked like, a large gray shed.

All heads turned and conversations ceased as they entered the small bar, and Coigne led Norma toward the dining area. Her eyes needed to adjust to the dim lighting. She almost tumbled over a shaggy dog the size of a love seat. The décor was simple— lanterns, anchors, netting, and a large, backlit aquarium filled with exotic fish.

"What's that, Coigne?" Norma asked, pointing at the fish. "Menu options?"

"Good evening." They were greeted with a big smile. "Booth or table?"

Norma eyed the name tag of the hostess, a cute teenager with round brown eyes and bangs, weighing all of ninety-eight pounds. "Miranda, I've always wanted to know. Does anyone ever prefer a table over a booth, in your experience?"

The girl said, "You'd be surprised, ma'am. Some people don't want the booth because they don't like their knees touching the other person's under the table."

"We'll take a booth," Norma said, then blushed as she realized Coigne would think she wanted to knock his knees. She snapped at Miranda, "We're just having pizza. Make it a large, with everything."

"Two Cokes, Miranda. And please say hello to your dad. Hope your mom's doing the cooking and not him."

"You got that right."

Over their drinks they examined the shark charm again. "What does it tell you, Norma?"

"For one thing, it's proof positive your staff sucks. Why was I the one to find it? Katepoo and his buddies were milling around long before I arrived."

He took the charm from her and held it close to the small lantern on the table. "I take it you found this somewhere Jimmy Katepoo should have?"

"I don't know who had searched the room, but someone had. It was taped off. They should have spotted it. I'd say that's sloppy, and when there's time we can talk about how there must be some basis other than intelligence and experience on which hiring decisions get made in your shop, but for now—"

"Do you think maybe the room was cordoned off because Katepoo had already found the shark and left it in place for me to see?"

"Do you?" Norma had to admit that thought hadn't occurred to her until now.

"Sometimes, Norma, a little reflection prevents reaching wrong conclusions about people."

"Not often."

"I'll start." Norma kept chewing while she recited. "Shark-park. We've already looked into the park possibility. "Dark-lark-bark."

"Bark." Coigne sounded hopeful. "Do you think the shark was a reference to your dog Barclay? You called him Bark, didn't you?"

"Yes, but that's too far-fetched.

"No pun intended. This is good. Let's keep going."

"And stop being a cheerleader. It's insidious."

"It's funny you say cheerleader, because I had an idea before we tried your phonetic/word association approach." Coigne finished his soda and set his glass down. "Isabella Miller, Laney's friend. She and Laney were playing a similar kind of rhyme game at the Postal I Scream place. Maybe the charm will mean something to her."

Norma was skeptical. Laney and Isabella hadn't been close friends. So far as she knew, they'd only gotten together once, the day Laney disappeared. Besides, the charm belonged to Gin. How could they have a common point of reference about Laney's mother's shark charm? Still, another trip to the Miller house wouldn't take long and it wasn't as though they had a long list of promising options.

Mr. Miller barely acknowledged their presence when he answered the door. His wrinkled dress shirt was unbuttoned and his undershirt in desperate need of bleach. Norma thought by comparison she looked pressed and tailored. His eyes were bloodshot and his face chalky, as though he'd been locked in a closet since their last visit. He said, "I can't imagine what more we can tell you. You're going in circles and frankly I don't have time for it."

Norma hated when people said "frankly" because the word always preceded a lie. Why didn't they just tell the lie?

With as much ill-grace as his body could convey, Miller led them into his living room.

"That's how an investigation works, Mr. Miller," Coigne said, using the voice of reason. "We won't take much of your time. Actually, it's Isabella's time we need. She here?"

"Oh for crying out loud. I'll see if she's awake." He left them, his shoulders slumped as though his burdens surpassed human endurance.

Despite his belligerence, Miller seemed to have less confidence than he did on their previous visit. Norma wondered why. She whispered to Coigne, "7:30 and no sign of the missus, and only one car in the driveway."

Coigne nodded. When Miller returned with his daughter, alert and fully dressed, Coigne smiled at her and said to Miller, "We were hoping to speak with Mrs. Miller, too. Would you mind getting her while we speak to Isabella?"

"She's not here," Isabella said.

At the same time her father said, "She's asleep."

Coigne looked from daughter to father.

"Oh that's right," Miller amended. "She's out. You know, ladies' night out." Miller shot his daughter a look that brooked no correction. "Anyway, we can tell you all there is to know."

"That's all right," Coigne said. He pulled the shark figure from his pocket and held it in his palm.

Norma watched Isabella closely. She could swear the girl had a reaction.

"That means nothing to me. Whose is it?" Miller asked.

"It belongs to Laney Sager's mother. We think Laney and her mother may be together, and Laney intentionally left it behind when she moved from one location to another. We hope she did that to give us some direction where to look for her. Maybe it brings something to mind in someone Laney's age. Isabella?"

"Look, Lieutenant Coigne. Kidnapping, murder, these are things we know nothing about. Do we look like people at home with the underworld?" Miller gestured toward his furnishings, drapes, pictures, all proof positive they were above the criminal classes. While Miller continued listing all the murky things the Millers didn't know about, Norma continued to study Isabella. Far from the spunky, smart girl who had greeted them on their last visit, Isabella remained silent during her father's blustering. Norma wondered if "Mom" had had enough of her blowhard husband and left Isabella to deal with him.

Coigne turned to the girl. "Any ideas?"

She picked up the shark and quickly gave it back. She shook her head.

"Okay." Coigne smiled and stood. Norma wanted to press harder, but followed Coigne's lead to the front door. Miller had gotten Coigne out the door and had almost nudged Norma through when she said in a stage whisper to Isabella, "Would you mind showing me to the ladies' room?"

Five minutes later, Norma opened the passenger door to Coigne's cruiser. "Well, if a grunt means farewell, Mr. Miller said, 'Farewell.' Oh, and by the way, Coigne, do one of those three-point turns you're so proud of and head us to the high school, whose sports teams are known as the —guess what?"

"Red Raiders."

"No. Red River's team *was* the Red Raiders. But when the school merged with Cockle Cove, whose team was the Blue Fins, they became a regional school with an entirely new team name. "

"The Sharks?"

"Ding-ding-ding. $200.00."

"So why couldn't the girl just say so?"

"All she said by way of explanation was, her father doesn't want the family to get mixed up in anything. I think he's mixed up, period. Also, Isabella confirmed Mom's 'away.'"

"Norma?"

"What?"

"Good idea, getting her to show you to the bathroom."

"Good idea questioning her in the first place. Now stop driving like your grandmother and get us to the high school."

32

"You can't mean Gin's involved."

Trooper Katepoo had phoned Anne Sager with the news that her daughter was most likely being held with Laney by Rahul Singh. He needed her to confirm that Gin owned a silver shark charm for a necklace or bracelet, but at the same time informed her the forensics left little doubt that Laney and her mother were together at the East Nauset Fish Pier the night before.

Despite an initial shock, Anne experienced the first bit of hope that her granddaughter might yet be saved. Gin was inept and selfish, but surely if she was with Laney she would do everything she could to protect her. Wouldn't she?

The more she thought about it, the less Anne felt surprised Gin was involved in Laney's disappearance. Her generalized suspicions were aroused the moment her daughter showed up hanging on the arm of cover boy, Ken Crawford. Her daughter expected her to believe that she had cleaned herself up because she'd found someone to love and was experiencing a belated convulsion of maternal longing. Gin supposedly saw Laney now as a "vital part" of her life, rather than an annoying drag on her chaotic existence. Once Gin saw that Anne wasn't going to roll over and let her have Laney, she must have found another way to get whatever it was she was after. That she'd put her daughter in harm's way wouldn't matter to Gin.

During their phone call, Trooper Katepoo said that Gin might be as much a victim as Laney, but Anne resigned herself to the more likely truth. Failing to get Laney legally, Gin was working with this gangster Rahul Singh to get what she was after.

She needed time to think and ended her call with the young trooper abruptly. She'd been homebound since Laney's disappearance except for her meeting at Coigne's office, and felt like she was losing her mind. If only Norma and Coigne would find Laney soon.

She headed for the beach, letting the local police officer stationed in her driveway know how to reach her.

Normally stamped with cheerful sailboats this time of year, the horizon was an uncompromised black line. An elderly couple gathered their beach blankets and umbrellas and made for home. The beach was empty.

Anne dropped her sandals and waded along the shoreline, her eyes trained on the foam. That's what had carried in Buddy Todd's body, a loser if there ever was one, a father who'd never paid one visit in all the years Laney had been in her custody. Anne supposed he'd been too busy touring rehab and penal facilities. He'd even been hospitalized from an overdose, according to Gin. How had Laney sprung from such rotten roots? Clearly, the girl hadn't inherited her intelligence from her father, although Gin was no genius either.

Anne stopped skipping rocks. For a long time she stared into the distance and finally sank to her knees. Her crazed howl blew clear across the Sound.

33

Isabella Miller was adept at slipping out of her house unnoticed. She'd escaped on many occasions, not for the usual mischief, but to hide out until the stinging barbs hurled between her parents had stopped. On her bike, she made it to the high school in twenty minutes. The sun wouldn't rise for hours. She hid her bike in back, double-checked her backpack for her cell phone and candy bars, and crept toward the front of the school. Coach Cummings would open the school and until then she'd stay hidden.

Laney's mom whimpered. With each curve along Route 28 her head lolled from side to side. She was almost unconscious. Even the car's rumbling over deep potholes didn't completely rouse her. Laney patted her mom's knee and tried to muffle her occasional moans with shushing sounds. Seated in the front passenger seat, Mr. Singh kept his gun aimed at her mom.

They would reach the high school soon and Laney still had only the vaguest of plans. She needed a way to ditch Mr. Singh and Varn and hide until either the men gave up and went away or help came, but she couldn't figure out how to protect her mom in the meantime.

The high school had seemed like a good place to lead her captors for the search of the letter for two reasons. For one, her mother's necklace brought to mind her school mascot and there was a slight chance someone looking for her might make the same connection. It was also all she had at hand to leave behind. For another, during orientation for entering the new high school after the merger, her class had trained to find good hiding places throughout the school in case of an active shooter.

Since she needed at least one good hideout for each class she might attend, she knew of many possibilities. There were the obvious places, inside a locker or a janitor's closet. She'd also tried out the movable aisles in the library. They were heavy to move on their tracks and there were many of them. Some of the bookshelves were empty and she'd succeeded in climbing on board and fitting her body snugly onto a shelf. But her idea for this emergency situation was to head for her hiding place in the gym.

She'd found it last winter when Aunt Norma took her to a basketball game. During halftime, she'd watched two workmen simply disappear. One minute they were crossing the gym floor close to the bleachers, and the next, they were gone. It was only at the end of the game when she was leaving that she heard a hissing noise like wood sliding on a metal track. The workmen reappeared. They'd re-entered the gym from behind a door that blended so well into the wall as to be practically invisible. Laney later figured out that the workmen used the hidden doorway to get behind the bleachers and service them.

Varn pulled the car into a secluded woods near the high school. "So how we gonna get inside without setting off alarms? The school must have security like a bank, Mr. Singh."

"You can't get inside now," Laney said. "You'll have to wait until it opens in the morning. The schedules are different in the summer."

Varn turned to Laney. "I didn't ask you, so shut up. We walk in and what, Mr. Singh? We see someone, we start shooting?"

"Not quite, Mr. Varn. Miss Laney and I will walk in when the school opens. That means we're going to sit in these woods quite some time. When we enter, I will explain that I'm with the FBI. I'll show them identification and say I'm helping Miss Laney retrieve important information from her locker and other locations, all relating to her recent frightening disappearance. Fortunately, I will not be concerned about cameras because I have a suitable disguise." Mr. Singh pulled from his jacket pocket a pair of dark sunglasses and an ear bud. He turned up his collar. "Miss Laney will of course back me up." Mr. Singh waited long enough for her to imagine the consequences if she did not, then he spelled it out for Varn. "If I do not return within, say, fifteen minutes, you are to leave, and when you get far enough away, deal with Gin. And I mean deal with her."

"Okay. You're the boss. But I don't like counting on the girl like this."

"What you like, Mr. Varn, is not relevant. Ever."

"Okay. Okay."

Laney was about to object to Mr. Singh's plan. She needed to keep her mom with her, but now saw Singh would never agree to let her accompany them into the school. He could hardly explain the limp woman to whomever they might run into and besides, he needed her mom held hostage so Laney would play along with his charade. She'd have to find a way to get help once inside the school, and hope it arrived in time to rescue her mom. She said, "We can get in as soon as Coach Cummings arrives. He's the athletic director and assistant principal. He's always the first one here and he unlocks the front door."

"That's more like it, Miss Laney. A little cooperation will help you and your mother." Singh turned the gun ever so slightly toward the girl. "But how do you know Coach Cummings' schedule and whether he follows it during the summer?"

Laney didn't need to prepare for Mr. Singh's question, only to tell the truth. "I'm lousy in gym, with pull-ups and rope climbing, things like that. I don't want to embarrass myself again next fall, so I've been coming in early for practice, before the day-camp programs and summer school start."

"You can't believe that, Boss."

She had to make Mr. Singh believe her. She would have to tell him the whole story about how her private athletic training came to be. "Coach Cummings is this odd-looking guy with these super wide hips and a pasty, pock-marked face and a lisp. Maybe that's why he did what he did for me that time he had us do pull-ups and push-ups. I was the only kid who couldn't do one. Not even one. No one said anything out loud, not at first, but I could hear the girls giggling behind my back. One girl even grunted as if she was trying to do a pull up, but it sounded like she was using the bathroom. Instead of drawing attention to me by yelling at the grunting girl, which is what I was afraid he'd do, Coach Cummings grabbed a basketball and did something amazing. He spun it on his finger for a long time, until everyone was looking at him, not at me. Then he put on this big globetrotter act, dribbling under his legs, passing to himself behind his back, all the while dancing around the gym floor, which astounded everyone because they used to imitate the way he teeter-tottered when he walked. They were as awful to him as they were to me. This time, though, everyone applauded like crazy. They'd forgotten about me. After class, he told me to come by the high school gym when school ended and he'd help me out. I've been practicing here most mornings ever since."

In the silence that followed, she wondered whether she'd even be in school next fall, much less build up her arm strength.

"That's a heartwarming story."

That was all Mr. Singh said, but he must have believed her. Later on, when she pointed to Coach Cummings' car and a man wearing a school T-shirt, shorts, and sneakers got out, Mr. Singh had them wait ten minutes before he and Laney shot across the athletic fields and entered the school.

34

Coigne could only describe his state of mind as goofball crazy. He'd once read about a guy whose beloved father was being eulogized at his memorial service and all the son could think of was outrageous raunchy sex. Back then, Coigne couldn't understand such a guy. Now he worried he was wired the same way. How could he be fantasizing about Norma, a more maddening, defiant creature he'd never known, at a time like this? He should be paying attention to his driving if he was going to career around corners like a drag racer. He should be calling for backup, and devising a strategy for rescuing the girl, if indeed she was at the high school. He had to wrestle his Norma fixation to the ground and get his mind back on the job.

They drove along Main past the library, an imposing, block-long stretch of white clapboard buildings, and swerved right onto Maple, then left on School. Coigne recalled the new $80 million school building had been controversial. Cockle Cove had overwhelmingly supported forming a regional school with Red River, but Red River rejected the merger a number of times, fearing the increased size of classes would cause SAT scores and college admission rates to suffer. Coigne hadn't paid much attention to size at the time, but now he had to. They were going to be searching for Laney inside the Titanic.

"Slow down, Coigne." They were about a hundred yards from the school. "I said, 'Slow down!'" Norma grabbed the steering wheel. "We just passed a parked car in the woods. Keep going, but slowly. Don't stop."

"Relax. I saw it. I'm going to overshoot the school so we get beyond the line of vision of anyone in that car. Then I'll turn into the school parking lot."

"Just do it."

Anyone could see how anxious Norma was. Coigne kept his voice calm. "We're going to have to wait until dawn. It's—"

"What? We can't wait."

"I was saying it's only a few hours away. We need light, Norma, or someone could get hurt. Even Laney, if she's here. When I get out, I'll circle behind the school on foot. The woods surround it and will give me enough cover. If there's anything going on, I'll call and let you know as soon as I can. I'll get backup and we'll take it from there. Norma, listen." He stopped talking until he had her full attention, her eyes on his. "You are to remain in the cruiser. This is an order. Do you hear me?"

"Fine."

"I'm serious, Norma. Promise."

"Promise."

Coigne pulled into the lot. They spoke every few moments about nothing in particular. Their eyes closed from time to time.

"Jesus, Norma, wait!"

The car door hung open. Norma had run toward the woods. Coigne swore out loud and fumbled for his cell. He made her out through the thick foliage, running along the phone perimeter of the school property. As he took off after her he gave instructions to Trooper Katepoo. She was already too far away for him to catch her. He could only pray she knew enough to stop and listen, a skill she'd never previously demonstrated.

He was glad it wasn't quite dawn, too early for morning joggers. The school would take about five minutes to circle, adding in extra time to get through the thicker scrub pines, and another minute to reach the hidden car.

He stopped when he spotted it. Norma had also slowed to a halt. He couldn't risk calling to her. The car's window might be open and any occupant would hear him. She started her approach like she was ducking a helicopter propeller. When she rose to peer inside the car, Coigne saw a flash of movement in the back seat. Gin Sager. Gun in the front seat! He flew at Norma and knocked her down. The car windows rolled down. He pulled Norma toward the rear of the car and shouted, "You are surrounded by state troopers. Throw your weapons outside the car." Silence. "You have no option but to—"

Commotion in the car. Coigne stood up to see Gin claw the driver's face.

"Shit!" from the driver.

Someone fired his gun. Norma rolled under the car. Gin fell back. More gunfire.

35

Laney was ashamed when she realized she was putting Coach Cummings in danger, but it was too late to turn back. With a silent prayer and firm push, she opened the front door to the school. The air was still and the entrance hall, silent. Laney figured Coach Cummings had already gone to his office off the gym.

Mr. Singh nudged Laney along and they arrived at the gym entrance. The lights were off. Laney peered through the morning haze to spot the "invisible door" near the bleachers. Just as she was about to enter the gym, Mr. Singh grabbed her wrist and squeezed so hard she couldn't move. They waited. She thought she heard a phone ring and Coach Cummings say hello, but she wasn't sure. More waiting. Her mind filled the void with echoes of sneakers squealing around the basketball hoops, referees blowing whistles, and crowds blasting out the command, "Shoot! Shoot!"

Music alerted them to Coach Cummings' location. He was singing random snatches of a song in his office. They stepped back into the shadow and waited. When he appeared, thank God he was wearing headphones and his back was to them. The sight of his boogey-walking would have been hilarious had she not been so afraid. It wasn't long before he returned to his office.

"Where do we go now, Miss Laney?" Mr. Singh again tightened his grip so she had to twist her body to avoid a broken wrist. "Where have you hidden the letter?"

She said nothing. What was there to say? She had no plan for reaching the invisible door. It was only about fifty yards away, but it may as well have been fifty miles. She'd stalled as long as she could.

In that moment she experienced what she'd only read about, resignation in the face of death. She wasn't fearful, nor did her whole life pass before her eyes. She was engulfed by sorrow, already in mourning for all the things she'd never do or say or feel. She turned to face Mr. Singh. "I can't—"

"GO SHARKS GO! GO SHARKS GO!" A thunderous noise exploded from all sides of the gym, like thousands of soldiers charging into the stands, their battle cry echoing from the rafters. Stomp-clap-stomp. Stomp-clap-stomp. "GO SHARKS GO! STRIKE THE BLOW! BEAT THE FOE! GO SHARKS GO!" Laney knew what was happening, but surprise loosened Mr. Singh's grip on her arm. Strobe lights flashed from a descending globe. She took her chance and bolted for the invisible door, got in and slid the door shut. Not once did she look back or even wonder why Coach Cummings had turned on the half-time cheer sequence. Behind the closed door, she struggled to breathe normally. Her breath seemed louder in that confined space than the roar of loyal fans.

Footsteps were getting closer. Was that the cheer sequence or Mr. Singh banging against the sliding doors? Someone was trying to find the opening. Gunfire? Yes. Scared beyond measure, Laney crawled deeper into the service space. The cheer sequence ended. Nothing. Then balls bouncing? Yes, a cascade of balls bouncing across the gym floor. Someone was getting pounded. Mr. Singh?

"Laney. Come out! It's me. Isabella."

36

Gin lay on her side, blood streaming from her bullet wound and spreading out beneath her clothes. She would have been surprised by its flow, a rill burbling over small stones. The look on her face was neither fearful, as might have been expected, nor peaceful, as might have been hoped. For once in her life she wore a look of purpose, determination, and courage. But the confusion all around her left no one free to observe how Gin Sager looked as she died.

"Stay down!" Coigne shoved Norma back. He fired again and retreated.

Coigne wasn't sure he'd gotten the driver. With a knee on Norma's back, he listened for movement, then whispered, "When I say go, you head through the woods the way you came. Get back to the car."

"I swear—"

"Do as I say or I'll kill you myself."

I may kill her either way. He scrambled crab-like to the driver's side of the car and listened, then looked in. Gruffly he called to Norma, "Go!" When he was sure Norma was far away he felt for Gin's pulse, then the driver's. He left them and ran toward the road. Thank God something was going right. Katepoo had arrived with his gun drawn.

The cruiser was unlocked and Norma got in. Despite rubbing her arms and rocking, she still shivered uncontrollably. As if banked for this occasion, she cried the tears of a lifetime. Her throat ached and her sweaty top clung to her skin. In her fury and dismay she slapped her tears away. What she'd done, thinking she should lead the rescue, perhaps getting Laney killed, putting Coigne's life at risk, was beyond forgiveness.

Coigne opened his cruiser door. Still rocking and crying, Norma hadn't heard him at first, but when she did she lunged and hugged him. "I'm so sorry."

"What's this? I can't understand you. You're sputtering."

"Laney. Is she all right? You could have been killed."

"Norma, Laney was—"

"No. No. No." She buried her face in his neck.

Coigne pulled her hands away and made her look at him. "Laney-was-not-in-the-car. It was Lancelot Varn and Laney's mother." He hesitated. "They are both dead."

Norma tried to stop her teeth from chattering. "Laney?"

"We think she's in the high school with Rahul Singh. Trooper Katepoo's here and I've got more troopers coming." He checked his watch. "We've got a few minutes." He pressed the all-door lock on his armrest.

Norma knew she had to say something about what she'd done. Coigne deserved to hear her admit to her own reckless, no, her outrageous behavior. But when she opened her mouth, no words would come.

Coigne stared ahead. Then, awkwardly, he leaned over and pulled her head onto his shoulder. "Okay. We'll get her back."

37

Barricades of vans, cruisers, and empty school buses surrounded the front and rear entrances to the school. Local police were stationed along the school's outer perimeter to redirect traffic. State troopers stood behind the front barricade, armed and padded so heavily they moved like robots.

Anne waited with Norma behind the barricades. Coigne had already told her Gin was dead. She knew she should be grieving. It was expected. But until she had Laney back she had no capacity for emotion. Her heart and mind were in lockdown.

Coigne explained he had remote access to the school intercom system and through it he would establish contact with Singh and negotiate for Laney's release. Anne almost expected Norma to criticize the extensive preparations before contact was to be made, but Norma only stared at the front entrance to the school.

Anne did the same. She knew she was probably imbalanced, thinking if they visualized the girl with enough detail and clarity, she would materialize. Nonetheless, with greater concentration than she'd ever mustered, she closed her eyes and summoned a picture of Laney, that shy smile, a vestige of her year with braces, those too-long, tanned legs, and that endearing, chest-hiding posture.

When Anne opened her eyes, Laney was standing at the entrance. Her face was bruised and caked with dried blood. Anne held her breath, not certain what she was seeing was real or imagined. Norma grabbed her hand and said, "She's standing. She's all right."

Beside Laney was a girl about her own age and a man in a Go Sharks! T-shirt. They looked disoriented, like they'd just been beamed down from a spaceship.

Coigne's voice blasted through his megaphone. "Stand down! Everyone stand down!" He walked slowly toward the school. The girls were arm in arm. When Coigne reached them, the odd group came together. When he turned around again, searching beyond the barricades, he gave Anne and Norma a thumbs-up.

38

That evening, Anne and Norma took turns sitting with Laney. She was taking the news of her mother's death harder than Anne had expected. She'd hoped to spare her granddaughter learning her mother had been shot to death, at least for that day. The girl had experienced enough trauma for a lifetime. But Laney's urgent pleas to see her mother and make sure she was safe were rising toward hysteria, and Anne couldn't lie to her.

Such agony over a mother who, for most of Laney's life, had shown little more than indifference, was beyond Anne's understanding. Maybe this was because her own sense of loss over Gin's death felt somehow muted. She'd prepared for Gin's premature death long ago and now was unable to experience heartbreak. The phrase that came to mind was "mourning lite," but Anne immediately regretted her flip play on words.

She stroked Laney's hair and whispered soothing sounds. It was sad that Gin wouldn't get a chance to make better choices for her life, but in her heart Anne doubted she would have done so had she lived. And just maybe the mourning lite idea had occurred to her because Gin's death might bring a new dawn for Laney.

Lieutenant Coigne was generous to provide her the details about Gin's final act of courage before Varn shot her. She'd attacked her captor with her fingernails, lacerating his retina and preventing him from getting a good shot off at Norma and the Lieutenant. Norma was riven with guilt for her indirect role in Gin's death, but in the end, it was better for Laney to see her mother in a heroic light than see her in jail. Anne believed that.

Dr. Zastinchek arrived that evening, coming all the way from Skaket to examine Laney in her own room. *A kindness unusual even for a pediatrician*, Anne thought. With her long blond hair held back by an early Hillary hair band, the young doctor looked more like Alice in Wonderland than a busy clinician. She left Laney's side only after completing her examination, prescribing counseling, and administering a mild sedative. She left a separate prescription for Anne. Within moments of closing her eyes, Laney slept, her breathing deep and steady.

"Surely it's obvious, Lieutenant Coigne. Rahul Singh killed Buddy Todd and Ken Crawford and if you catch Singh, case closed." Anne paused. "How in the world did he get away? And can we sit down? I'm so tired."

The effort of pulling out the piano bench and shifting it to face Coigne while he filled her in on the next steps in the investigation felt monumental, but the perch allowed Anne to hear if she was needed upstairs. Even with such proximity, she was glad Norma was up there with Laney.

"We'll be getting more details from Laney about the sequence of events inside the school, but until she's rested we'll have to piece together ourselves how Rahul Singh got away, Ms. Sager. As you could see, he wasn't with Laney, Miss Miller, and Coach Cummings when they came out of the building and none of them saw him leave."

"That means a killer is still on the loose and," she lowered her voice, "Laney could still be at risk."

Coigne did not to respond directly to the implication that his police work was faulty. "As for who killed Buddy Todd and Ken Crawford, we don't have proof Singh killed either one of them, although it's likely he killed Crawford. We've pieced together some background from Laney's story about the letter Singh was so desperate for, as well as Crawford's emails and texts. As co-owners of Red River Resort, Singh and Crawford were business partners, but behind each other's backs they were working against each other. Singh wanted that letter found and destroyed, but Crawford wanted to hold on to it. We believe Singh felt threatened by Crawford, who could potentially control the property through his marriage to Gin and her custody of Laney. Even if Laney's claim to the property wouldn't ultimately hold up, so long as Crawford could threaten to pursue it on Laney's behalf, he'd have effective control of the resort at a time when its net worth was about to skyrocket." Coigne explained to her the resort's development plans.

"I follow," Anne said.

"Laney's account supports this theory. She says her mother thought Singh killed Crawford and would kill them too if they couldn't come up with the letter. Gin was expecting to be rewarded by Singh if she helped *him* rather than her fiancé find the missing letter."

"That sounds about right," Anne said. "Gin must have figured cash in hand from Singh was easier than marriage, a custody battle, and maybe custody itself.

Coigne nodded, "We'll never know. But I can't see why Singh would kill Buddy Todd. Laney says Singh was hell-bent on finding the letter. What motive would he have to bump off the most direct link to the discovery of that letter, Buddy Todd?"

"Hm." Anne's hands began to move across her lap as though practicing chords and scales. "You may be right, but isn't it more likely Singh got fed up trying to get the location of the letter out of an uneducated, drug-saturated, ex-con—forgive me— and decided to try his luck with the beneficiary herself? A child is more malleable, more easily frightened into saying things. So he leapfrogged over Buddy Todd and went after Laney."

"By 'leapfrogged' you mean he murdered Buddy Todd. I think you're underestimating Rahul Singh, Ms. Sager. If he's anything, he's patient and calculating. It's how he built up his syndicate, victim by victim, industry segment by industry segment. Unless Rahul killed Buddy Todd by accident, and again, accidents don't fit Singh's profile, it was someone else. The clincher is that Singh's got an alibi. According to the medical examiner, Todd was drugged, then killed, about twenty-four hours before Laney found him. Singh only arrived at Logan from Heathrow the morning Laney found Buddy Todd. His sidekick, Lancelot, was with a prostitute for the time in question."

"I vote for Gin," Norma said, walking into the living room. "I'm sorry to say it, Anne, and I'm the last one who should say it, but if Gin knew about the letter from Crawford or Singh, take your pick, she'd want Buddy out of the picture, wouldn't she? Out of the competition for the spoils, something like that?"

"Come on, Norma." Anne shook her head. "Gin might well have thought about killing Buddy, but carry it out? I don't think she'd even know where to buy duct tape, much less wrap the man in it."

Coigne agreed. "To be willing to kill him, Gin would have to think Buddy didn't have the letter. Maybe she did, maybe she didn't. Guess I better try to find out." He stood. "You coming?"

"That's kind of you to ask," Norma said.

Anne could see that something had changed between Lieutenant Coigne and Norma. The ego-busting bombs Norma usually dropped on Coigne were still in their hold. Admittedly, Norma was shaken up by her ordeal at the high school, but still, Coigne had the reputation as a dirty cop. Norma had said so. If anyone was going to be subjected to Norma's withering attacks, it would be a guy who'd betrayed the public trust. So why did Norma suddenly sound like Emily Post?

Anne would have been gratified to learn that her best friend was at that moment asking herself the same question. Norma was having trouble reconciling the twaddle she'd picked up around town with what she'd learned about Coigne from her own experience with him. It wasn't his courage during the shoot-out that convinced her she might have made a mistake about him, although she had to admit the way he'd taken down Lancelot Varn, shooting the sonofabitch in the face through the open window, was impressive. He'd controlled his rage when he got back in his cruiser, resisted blasting her head off for risking everything, and even went so far as to reassure her about Laney. Was that the behavior of someone happy to take bribes from criminals? She needed some distance to get the question answered.

"You go ahead, Coigne. I'll stick with Anne. I want to be here when Laney wakes up. Would you get in touch if something happens?"

"Of course." On the verge of leaving, Coigne said, "I almost forgot. Our office tracked down Bradford Todd, Sr.'s will. It's fifteen years old, so Laney wasn't even born when he wrote it. It left everything he owned in trust for his first grandchild until he or she reached twenty-one, but only on the condition that the child was raised by his son and his son was, in so many words, clean, or raised by the child's natural mother under the same health conditions. If those conditions weren't met, any assets would go to his church."

"Okay," Norma said, taking a seat. "So what did he own when he died?"

"So far as we can tell, nothing."

Anne said, "Your theory, Lieutenant Coigne, must be that Todd, Sr. learns he has a granddaughter, probably from his son, and writes a letter to Buddy about the property he's leaving to Laney. Buddy doesn't get the letter or understand the letter while he's still in rehab or on the streets. Then he gets out of rehab and finds the letter."

Coigne nodded. "Go on."

"But why is the letter so important?" Anne asked. "If he died not owning anything, the letter would be moot. Isn't that the term, Norma?"

"By the time he died, he didn't have the property," Norma said, distracted.

"You all right, Norma?"

"Sorry, Coigne. A crazy thought occurred to me, but it's too soon to go public with it."

"What I can't figure out," Coigne continued, "is why Todd, Sr. sold the land to Red River Resort if he wanted his grandchild to inherit it. And by the way, where did the proceeds from the sale go?"

"Where indeed?" Norma said.

39

Lieutenant Coigne and Trooper Barbara Ferguson, new to the Cape and with a husband on duty in the Middle East, interviewed Laney at the Barracks with her grandmother present. Later they questioned Isabella Miller, accompanied by her father. In neither case was Coigne getting much to move the investigation forward and help him find Singh.

"Not surprising," Norma said when he called. "For most people the Barracks isn't conducive to vivid recall. And who speaks up in front of their parents anyway?" She thought a moment. "I have an oddball idea. Why don't you meet them at Postal I Scream? Laney will let you know if that venue makes her uncomfortable, since that's where her troubles began, but I have a feeling returning there might even start the healing process. Anyway, just a thought."

He might not be able to rely in court on anything that came out of an interview without parents present at a fast food joint, but that didn't worry him. He had enough from the Barracks interviews to tie up Rahul Singh for years to come. But he had to catch him first.

Side by side at Postal I Scream, the girls were striking in their youthful attractiveness and the differences between them. Where Laney was hazel-eyed and fair, Isabella's chestnut mane was tinged in copper. Where Laney was slender, all arms and legs, Isabella already had curves. Where Laney looked smart, but worried, Isabella looked bright and impish. If he knew anything about the world, these two would not wait long for a prom date.

He wondered what it must be like for Laney. It was only twenty-four hours since she'd been rescued. She looked dazed, and why not? She'd lost her mom and dad in a matter of days. He wasn't sure whether never having known her dad made the loss easier or harder to bear. She was luckier than some, though. Still had family, her grandmother, for one, and having Norma on her side was no small bonus.

Norma may have thought he asked her to join them for ice cream so the girls would feel at ease, but he also needed her insights. If not for her, they might not have found Laney in time.

At first she'd declined the invitation, saying she had something else important to look into. He assumed it had to do with the lawsuit against her. In the end she changed her mind and came along.

He couldn't help noticing, ever since the rescue, Norma's attitude toward him had changed. It wasn't that she'd warmed up. He wasn't deluded enough to think she'd ever actually give him a chance. But rather than the abrasive bull dog he'd come to know and love, she acted puzzled.

As for what Norma had done at the high school, she'd gone beyond the pale in recklessness, no question about it. But she was sorry. He doubted she would walk the straight and narrow ever after and a part of him hoped to God she wouldn't. He'd had plenty of explaining to do to the district attorney, but finding Laney safe, and convincing the DA Norma had been vital to that outcome, saved Coigne's neck and hers.

Norma was talking with the girls, not as though she were their age, but as though they were hers. They laughed, enjoying her company. Even beside their flowering prettiness, Norma's character and beauty left them in the dust. Something about her looked different today. He'd had no idea she had nice legs until she came through the door of Postal I Scream in a knee-length skirt. Not that he was into fashion, but on her, the skirt, a sort of poodle skirt without the poodle, worked with her Bite Me shirt. And her hair. She was wearing it loose, not bundled under that hat. It was that golden color of beach grass in the fall.

He was not so smitten as to be blind to her physical quirks. Like when she was trying to make a decision, she'd make quick jerks with her head like a little bird. But such a flaw, on Norma, was adorable. Maybe he was too smitten.

The girls opted for scoops in cups rather than cones, probably because they'd ordered four scoops apiece. They were having fun and the whole scene jarred with the questions Coigne needed to ask. He got started.

Laney answered his questions, taking them through the chase on the bike path, to the cottage in the woods, then the fish pier and finally the high school. Much of what she said he already knew, but was hoping he'd missed something.

"When I got to the high school," Laney said, "I was all out of ideas. If it hadn't been for Isabella—"

"I'm just glad I got there in time." Isabella beamed in the limelight. "When Ms. Bergen asked me about sharks and I told her about the high school mascot, I let it go at that, at first. But after she left, I started thinking about what I would do in Laney's place. How would I get away from a kidnapper? I knew Coach Cummings opened the school early in the summer. I've been taking biology in summer school so I don't have to take it in the fall. So I hid outside at the school until he arrived."

"Did your parents let you go there by yourself?" Laney asked.

"Well, not exactly."

Coigne knew Isabella had snuck out without her father's knowledge because he later caught a raft of shit from Miller for "inducing my daughter to risk her life."

"But Isabella, I still can't figure out how you turned on the public address system," Norma said.

"I didn't turn it on. When I saw Coach Cummings go into the building, I called the school with my cell phone. I got lucky. He picked up. I told him I'd just seen Laney and a man go into the building and he could be the kidnapper. Good thing he'd seen on the news that Laney was missing or he would have thought I was nuts. He left his gym office and went to look at the security cameras. He got back to the phone and said he'd seen Laney and a man right outside the gym and he'd call the police and I was to go right home. But I had an idea. I told him about the half-time cheer."

"But why did he play the cheer? Why wouldn't he just wait for the police?" Coigne knew the answers from his interview with Cummings but wanted Isabella's version.

"I had the idea in the first place because I thought it would be better if Laney were not so close to Mr. Singh when the police came. What if he used her as a hostage so he could get away? I was hoping she'd run when the strobe lights started. Coach Cummings agreed with me."

"Right. Oh, Iz. You were so right!"

Laney's love for her new friend reminded Coigne of the name of the church he grew up in, Our Lady of Perpetual Adoration. If Isabella ever needed someone to lay down her life for her, Laney would be first in line.

Isabella licked the ice cream off her spoon, turning it upside down. "At first Coach was worried the noise might frighten Mr. Singh into hurting Laney, but we figured we had no choice. He was going to hurt her anyway."

"Right!" Laney said again, nodding. Laney's color was now high, any trace of worry erased by the warmth of friendship.

It made Coigne smile, whether at the resilience of youth or the image of Singh startled by the noisy cheer, he wasn't sure. He took a few bites as Isabella continued.

"I couldn't help myself. I had to come in and see if I could help. As soon as I walked down the hall I heard the cheers. I flattened myself against the wall and crept down to the gym. I guess Laney had already hidden behind the bleachers because Mr. Singh was darting back and forth trying to figure out where she'd disappeared to. Somehow in that strobe light I made it to Coach Cummings office, but Mr. Singh got off a shot. I don't know if he was aiming at me or what. Anyway, Coach Cummings saved the day. When that shot was fired he came tearing out of his office fully armed. You should have seen him. He had this storage bin full of basketballs and he started pelting Mr. Singh. Boom! Boom! His head, his feet, one right in his face. It was beautiful. Knocked him flat on his back. That's when he lost his gun and ran."

"All three of you were heroes," Coigne said.

Before long, the conversation turned to summer plans, new movies, and the cataclysmic break-up of Skyler and Amelia, whoever they were.

He needed to tax Laney with a question more difficult than the preceding ones. When the girls had finished their ice cream and wiped their mouths, they looked up. "What we don't know, Laney, is what became of Mr. Singh. It's important we find him. Very important that—"

"Because you think he'll come after me again?"

No more face aglow. He'd blown it.

Norma pushed her dish aside. "No, not likely at all he'll come after you. Listen, kid. He knows you'll be watched round the clock. He's not going to try anything. Am I right, Coigne?"

"Right!" he said. They all laughed because he sounded like Laney. But the truth was, Singh could still be after the letter and Laney. She was an eyewitness he couldn't afford to leave alone, but Coigne wasn't going to say so. "We're trying to find him because he may have been directly involved in two murders and—we know he was in part responsible for a third." He didn't want to bring up her mother, but she was too perceptive for him to sugarcoat realities. Norma helped him out again.

"Under the law, Rahul Singh is as guilty of your mother's murder as if he pulled the trigger himself."

"When we catch him," Coigne said, "we'll have him put away forever. So whatever you remember, anything he might have said about where he was headed will help."

Laney looked wary, but seemed calm enough for him to continue. He explained that Singh had left on foot, but the canine unit lost his trail as soon as he made it to Route 28, about a mile from the school. Police officers waited at Red River Resort, but Singh was a no-show. BOLOs, or Be-on-the-Lookout alerts, were cast wide, as Singh had lots of connections. All modes of transportation for getting off the Cape were under close watch.

"He just wanted to talk about the letter and where it was hidden," Laney said. "He never raised his voice or hit me, not like that nutcase, Varn, but he was even more of a maniac. Like he'd die if he didn't get that letter."

Coigne tried to keep it light, but the questions he needed answered didn't help. "Did you suggest to him any possible hiding place other than the high school? If you did, it's conceivable he'd head there—"

"Why would Singh still be looking elsewhere for the letter?" Norma crushed her empty ice cream cup. "He obviously bought Laney's story that it was hidden in the high school, or they wouldn't have gone there."

She had a point, but Coigne had one, too. "Maybe he's in the same spot we're in, 'eliminating a multitude of locations.'" He looked sideways at Norma to see if she recognized the reference. She rolled her eyes to say she did. "And he may be hoping Laney lied about the high school, to stall for time, which she did. A brave and brilliant move, I might add."

Laney smiled.

"He's right, Laney," Isabella chimed in. "I never would have thought of it, especially if I were scared."

"We have no promising clues on his whereabouts, so we take what we've got and run with it."

"You're ever the optimist, Coigne," Norma said. "But it seems like a colossal waste—"

"I think he did figure out I was bluffing, Aunt Norma." Laney spoke slowly, as if mentally replaying a scene. "Right before the cheer began, when we were standing in the doorway to the gym, I was out of ideas and gave up. Mr. Singh knew I had given up."

Coigne gave her a moment. "What makes you say that?"

"He had me by the wrist." She gripped her wrist to demonstrate. "And even though I wasn't pulling away, his grip kept getting tighter and tighter, not because he was trying to hold onto me, but to punish me for fooling him. And to answer your other question, Lieutenant Coigne, I never suggested any other hiding place. And my mom didn't either, even though they tried to make her." She closed her eyes. They all waited, and Coigne wished they could erase her dark memories. When a tear rolled down her cheek, Isabella placed an arm around her shoulders.

Coigne looked around, worried he'd caused customers to stare at Laney and she'd be self-conscious once she looked up, but the tables were full of people 100 percent absorbed in their own dramas. "What you've told us is very helpful, Laney. Rahul Singh has no leads from you or your mom, so he'll use the same tools for finding the letter that we'll use for finding him—logic. Right now he's wondering where you might have hidden it. We're a step ahead of him, because we know you'd never even heard about it, much less hidden it. But he doesn't believe that. From what you've told us, he believes you know exactly where it is."

Laney nodded and wiped her cheek with her napkin.

"Now. Everyone. Who has a suggestion?" Coigne looked from face to face. "Where would Mr. Singh think Laney hid the letter?"

Isabella said, "You mean we have to get inside Singh's head? That's foul."

Laney said, "It's revolting!" The girls burst out laughing and Laney's bad moment evaporated.

Norma leaned forward, both elbows on the table. "The obvious place she'd hide it…." She sat back and caught Coigne's eye. "Well, there is no obvious place. Let's stop playing this dumb game."

He knew what she was thinking and could have kicked himself for starting down this path. The obvious place was in Laney's home. You hide things where you can get at them but where no one else can. And he also knew why Norma stopped. Yes, they were only speculating, but the last thing Laney needed to worry about was Rahul Singh invading her home and disposing of her and her grandmother while he ransacked the house.

"Norma's right. It's my job to figure this out. The only job these girls have right now is to enjoy the rest of their summer." He tapped the side of his head with one finger. "I have a thought. I don't suppose you two would like a boat ride with the harbormaster? I mean, speaking of sharks, I hear some have been spotted off Monomoy."

"Are you kidding?" Isabella said. "Could we?"

"I could find out. The harbormaster is an old buddy of mine and he owes me."

"Good idea, Coigne. Ladies, go use the restroom. This may be your last chance for a stationary ride, if you know what I mean."

"Aunt Norma—you're bad."

"So they say."

Once the girls left, Norma tossed her napkin on the table and searched her purse for car keys.

Coigne said, "I'll see if my buddy will keep the girls occupied while we bring Anne Sager up to speed and tighten security at her house. You going on the boat ride?"

"I would, but I have a little breaking and entering to do."

"Please don't tell me." Coigne started to rise, but Norma grabbed his arm.

"Do you really think Singh is still looking for Laney and that damn letter?"

Coigne studied Norma's eyes, assessing whether to confide in her his worst fears. "Yes, I do. Our intel is that Singh is the big boss, but he's by no means the biggest boss. Anyone else would drop the hunt at this point, but Singh has to keep the search going, or face the consequences."

"Just be careful, Will." Norma jumped up, overturning her chair and making a cacophonous racket. Everyone stared. She stared back. "Gotta problem?"

40

Having just paid a visit to Dunscombe and Dohnan, Norma had no trouble remembering directions to the law firm. At least she wouldn't meet up with Dohnan's obsessive timekeeping receptionist—Carl Somebody— although she did feel sorry for getting him fired on account of her last visit.

The parking lot was empty but for one car, Dohnan's. She'd never actually seen his car, but she knew this was his. A lawyer on the Cape with any sense would strive to avoid driving around town in a flashy car. Forget *Lincoln Lawyer*. And forget what goes on in the big cities like New York. Around here, flaunting wealth only serves to remind everyone how outrageous lawyers' rates are. No one should make so much money by simply getting into arguments. Obviously, the red Viper in the lot belonged to Mr. Indiscretion himself. And if the car's conspicuousness didn't give Dohnan away, the vanity plates, "THRLRBLS," were proof positive.

With Dohnan on the premises, Norma's hopes of sneaking in undetected were thwarted, but she stuck with her plan. What she was about to dish out, Dohnan had coming to him. She rattled the front door knob. Locked. She knocked. No one came, so she removed her shoe and started banging.

"…break the door down or what?" Dohnan had started yelling before he'd opened the door. He looked like he'd been working out. His forehead shined like it was coated in baby oil and he wore a white clingy V-neck, exposing moist fur and a hint of cleavage.

"I'm tied up, Norma."

"I wish you were."

"I thought our business had concluded. Make an appointment with my receptionist on Monday. I believe you've met him."

"Oh, Carl is back? I thought you'd fired him."

"Goodbye, Norma." Dohnan got ready to slam the door, but Norma was an expert at getting a foot in the door, literally. She'd worked her way through college selling magazines. The technique gave her enough time to say, "I know about Bradford Todd's letter."

Dohnan took his bluster down a notch. "Let's make this quick, Norma. I told my wife I'd be home in an hour." They headed down the hall and he opened the door to his office. As she'd remembered, there was a treadmill in the corner and the room smelled like B.O.

"I'm sure your wife's used to your prolonged absences, although it saves time having Bitty Booty's law office right down the road."

Dohnan spun around. "What the hell are you talking about? I thought you wanted to discuss—"

"Calm down, Thriller Balls. The fact that your wife made the sad mistake of marrying a pig isn't my problem."

Dohnan slammed his fist on his desk. "Just say what you have to say and get out."

Spit bubbled in the corners of Dohnan's mouth. It was time to get to the point. She avoided taking a seat in front of his desk and opted for the round conference table by the window, where he joined her. She figured she may as well give passersby a good look at them both in case he slugged her and she needed a witness.

"I thought you were trying to squeeze me for damages with that frivolous lawsuit," she began, "dreamed up no doubt while helping your nephew, Carl, hone his creative notary skills. Yessiree, it does pay to have a notary in the family when your lawsuit hinges on the fraudulent signature of a dead person. Don't deny it. I've already checked it out."

"How dare you insinuate I was guilty of malfeasance when you're the one—"

"Even your attempt to have me perjure myself wasn't the real reason you threatened me with that lawsuit. I'm ashamed to say I missed the real reason. It was so simple."

"All right, Norma. I'll play the game. Anything to get you out of here. Why did I threaten you with a lawsuit?"

Norma let him twist in the breeze. She was comfortable, seated in a swivel-tilt leather chair, the kind that starts at about four grand. She rocked back and forth, a girl with all the time in the world. "You'll be glad to know that Bradford Todd's granddaughter, Laney, was found alive and well and talking about a letter written by her grandfather, Old Man Todd. It seems young Laney was to inherit valuable property that somehow got sold to those nice felons at Red River Resort. Say. Isn't that the same property *you* sold on Old Man Todd's behalf to the resort? I seem to remember reading something about that in your files. I ask myself, 'Why would Old Man Todd sell property to Red River Resort when he'd intended it for his granddaughter?' And then I figured it out. He didn't sell it. *You* did. And he didn't even know you'd sold it. According to this letter everyone's wild to get their hands on, he intended the property for his grandchild. You are clever, Dohnan."

"Why are you bothering me with this pathetic accusation? The guy was senile. He'd been senile for years. Everyone knows that. He probably wrote a hundred letters about his intentions. So what?"

"Really, Dohnan. Hyperbole makes you sound desperate. And wipe your mouth." She made a face and pushed a box of Kleenex toward him. "You've got foam."

She gave him a moment to absorb what he'd just said, but it was clear he wasn't getting it. "Listen, brain-dead cretin, you signed conveyance documents on Old Man Todd's behalf in the sale of Samoset Way beach access to Red River, and you did so with a general power of attorney executed at about the same time. Remember, I've been through your files. If he was senile for years, your POA was no good and the sale was no good."

"He wasn't nuts when he sold the property. The old man went senile a year or so after the sale. That's probably when he wrote whatever letter you're talking about."

"Do your homework. He died just a week after the sale, which is an interesting coincidence, but we'll leave that well-timed death for another day. Admit it. He never knew you sold the property out from under him, although he probably suspected you were a thief or he would have copied you on his letter to Buddy."

"Nonsense! When we sold the property to Red River Resort, he forgot he'd intended the property for his grandchild, or he changed his mind."

"I have another explanation." Norma stopped rocking. "You didn't know he'd written the letter. Somewhere along the line Old Man Todd stopped trusting you. Anyway, he was too busy dying of cancer to notice when you sold his property. I guess you didn't want to worry him about it, huh?"

Dohnan grabbed his car keys and leaned forward. "You're nuts, Norma. Those sale documents are all properly signed and witnessed."

"No doubt by your no*tari*ous nephew, Carl, which would explain his guaranteed for life employment."

"None of this is any of your business."

"What a shock it must have been for you when Mary Temple sold away her interest in Red River Resort, after all the trouble you'd gone to for her sons. Hope they hadn't already paid you, but perhaps they didn't have to. Bank records will show where proceeds from the sale of Samoset Way wound up."

"You want to talk about senile, Norma, let's talk about it. Mary Temple had no idea she was practically giving away her Red River interest, and her sons had every right to be upset when she sold it. Talk about malpractice; overlooking that right of first refusal language was a doozy."

"Doozy. Legal term? And that brings me back to *why* you threatened to file the lawsuit.

"Dear God, why *did* I threaten to file the lawsuit?"

"Same reason you ransacked my home."

"Why?"

"You drafted suit papers simply so I'd gather my files in one place for review. For all you knew, they were kept offsite with a record storage company. That's what most lawyers do with their closed files. You needed all my files, computer documents and hard copies, where you could get at them. You tossed my home, or had someone do it for you, because somehow you knew I represent Anne Sager in all her affairs, and she might have given me a copy of Old Man Todd's letter. Buddy Todd, fresh out of rehab, found the letter and made the mistake of confronting you about selling off his dad's property, which, by the way, gives you a damn solid motive for murdering him. You weren't sure I had a copy, but you couldn't take a chance that *I'd* get hold of it, because I might wonder, just like I'm doing now, why the same property intended for Todd's granddaughter was sold to Red River Resort. You had to search my files and my house, and destroy my computer, too. By the way, every good attorney makes a backup. Make a note of that."

"No one will believe you, Norma." Dohnan was doing some heavy breathing and he wasn't even on the treadmill. "First of all, you don't represent Anne Sager in all her affairs. She uses Bitty Booty, that is, Bitty Buchanan for these types of matters, so why would I want to go through *your* files? Where's the motive? I'd ransack Anne Sager's files, or Bitty's, not yours."

"You would have ransacked Anne's files, only she's had state troopers crawling all over her place since the Buddy Todd drowning. And as for Bitty, I'm sure you've searched every inch of her."

"That's it. I've had enough." Dohnan lifted his windbreaker off its hook and charged toward the door.

He did look beaten up, but Norma wasn't through with him yet. She reached into her bag. "Don't go yet." She turned on her cell phone and clicked. "You shouldn't have asked for that second scotch." They both then listened to the video recording.

"We're not asking you for much. We're simply asking you not to contradict us if you're called as a witness against Red River Resort for swindling Mrs. Temple out of her partnership interest. In return, we won't sue you for overlooking the right of first refusal provision."

"Of course they didn't swindle her out of her interest. You're asking me to lie under oath. This sounds like extortion and suborning perjury. Am I on the right track?"

"That's the idea."

When Norma stopped the video, she said, "I already sent this to the DA, so don't get stupid. I don't care whether or not you swindled Old Man Todd. The law will catch up with you. I do care that you killed my dog. I'll do everything in my power to make sure you're convicted of Buddy Todd's murder."

"For God's sake, Norma. Where do you get this stuff?"

"You had plenty of motive. You had to silence Buddy."

"I'm going to say this once. *I never killed anyone.* You start spreading that rumor around and I may have to amend that statement. Now get the hell out."

Norma headed down the hallway with Dohnan close on her heels. She'd hoped to see more signs of guilt when she accused him of murdering Buddy Todd and was disappointed to find none. But something he'd said wasn't sitting well with her. Not well at all.

41

Coigne left Postal I Scream, cell phone pressed to his ear. Trooper Katepoo was letting him know a call had come in from a Louise "Wheezy" Wickersham.

"I know who she is. I ran into her the day Laney Sager discovered the body on the beach. She's the kind who thrives on another's adversity, and probably causes it."

"She says she's seen a stranger around Samoset Bluff Lane who, I think, fits the description of Rahul Singh."

"Good. Her call might confirm what I think Singh's up to."

Coigne filled Katepoo in on his conversation with Norma about the likelihood Singh would search the Sager house for the letter. They agreed to meet at Sandy's Hardware Store near Samoset Way and come up with a plan.

He reached Anne Sager to get permission for Laney to go out with the harbormaster and while at it, asked her to contact Miller to get permission for Isabella. Coigne figured the guy would be less likely to say no if Anne did the asking. Cowardly, true, but Coigne didn't feel the need to waste courage on someone like him.

He was glad to have young Katepoo on the case. Other guys chided Jimmy for his stilted manner and lack of interest in blow-by-blow recaps of ball games and hot dates, but Coigne valued his dedication and willingness to learn.

Sandy's Hardware Store was a small white clapboard building in the shade of a gnarled oak tree on Route 28. The black paint on the storefront sign had peeled so badly all you could see was ndy's ardwa Sto. The display window was filled with small appliances and tools dusty enough to have sat there since 1950. The store opened during the summer and made one or two sales a week at prices so high, in Coigne's opinion, one or two sales was enough.

Trooper Katepoo pulled in and crossed the gravel drive to Coigne's cruiser. The young man immediately laid out the plan he'd devised on the way over.

"The problem for the suspect is to get into Sager's without attracting attention. I noticed when we were first working on the Buddy Todd murder that one side of the Sager house is completely hidden behind this huge wall of rhododendrons. It's a good fifteen feet high." He stretched his arm above his head. "And it's a solid green wall. Behind it are Bilco doors that open onto a stairway to the basement. Singh will figure his best bet for getting into the house undetected is behind that green wall. We call Ms. Sager and have her "accidentally" leave the Bilco doors unlocked. When Singh searches for an entrance he sees the Bilco doors, opens up, and climbs down the stairs. We're there to welcome him."

Katepoo waited for Coigne's reaction. All that eagerness didn't mean the plan would work, but the young man had taken initiative and in Coigne's book that counted.

"Think about details. Assuming you're right and Singh is staking out the house, how do *we* get into the house and down to the basement without Singh spotting *us*?"

"Ms. Sager unlocks the Bilco doors, we scoot behind the green wall and through the doors ourselves. Then we wait."

"How about the fact that I had Trooper Ferguson stay with Ms. Sager today? Barb Ferguson's been there since this morning, cruiser sitting in the driveway. Won't that tend to discourage Singh from making his move to your green wall?"

"I'd forgotten that." Only slightly discouraged, Jimmy Katepoo looked away to consider the new problem. "Her being there is actually helpful, sir. Assuming Singh's watching the house, we can control the timing of his move if we call Barb,

Trooper Ferguson, and have her make a big deal of leaving the house so Singh sees the coast is clear. Meanwhile, with all that action in the driveway, that's when we slip behind the green wall and into the basement and wait, but not for long. Trooper Ferguson drives off, Singh sees his chance, creeps around to the side of the house and down the basement stairs and he's done."

Coigne nodded, then cocked his head. "And what about Anne Sager?"

"Sir?"

"What's she doing while all this is happening in her basement?"

"Oh. Right. We've put her in danger by sending Trooper Ferguson away and luring Singh to the house. In that case, Anne Sager should leave with Ferguson."

"Yes, that's exactly what she should do."

Katepoo's plan was sound because it was simple, depending primarily on Singh's being in the neighborhood and willing to believe the Bilco doors were left unlocked accidentally. Summertime on the Cape, not implausible. But there was one more person who needed to be placed out of harm's way, far from the house when Singh showed up. Coigne hated to do it, but didn't see a choice. He liked Jimmy and wanted to reward his taking the initiative, but wouldn't risk him on a dangerous stake-out. He took a deep breath. "Last problem to solve, Trooper. If Singh breaks free, I need a back-up, someone who can catch him if he's flushed out the front door."

Katepoo said nothing, but Coigne read disappointment in the sag of his shoulders. "Ferguson will still be out with Ms. Sager, obviously. Right now, you're all I've got."

The young man closed his eyes, as if willing Coigne not to say what he was about to say.

"I need you to hang back, because you're faster than I am and can probably outrun Singh. I'll take the basement post alone."

Still the younger man said nothing.

"You cool with that?"

"Sir."

Coigne knew it could be a long time before Jimmy Katepoo wanted to work with him again.

They figured out the location where Katepoo could best watch the Sager house, Norma's driveway, and Coigne said he'd give her a call.

"Do you need to ask permission?"

"This may come as a surprise to someone as dedicated as you, Trooper, but some people don't fancy the possibility of a shoot-out in their driveway. Besides, we need her to steer clear of home until everything is over." As it turned out, he had to leave a voicemail.

Katepoo got through to Ferguson and they set the plan in motion.

"It will only take a couple of hours, Ms. Sager. I'll have you back by dinnertime. I promise."

Coigne took his cue from Barb Feguson's loud voice in the driveway to start moving toward the green wall. He felt he'd missed something in planning and gave fleeting thought to abort, but in the excitement he forgot all about it.

"Fine." Ms. Sager opened the cruiser door and got in. There must have been more conversation in the car because she got out again. "I *have* to have them. I never go anywhere without my sunglasses. If you hadn't hurried me, Trooper Ferguson, I wouldn't have forgotten them. Anyway, I'll be right back."

Coigne was satisfied with the performance. It rang true. A patient officer of the law was gently coaxing cooperation out of her charge and that charge was sounding annoyed at having to do something for her own good. If Singh were anywhere close by, he'd know his best chance for searching the house was as soon as the two women pulled out of the driveway.

The light from the small basement windows allowed Coigne to look around without using an artificial light source. He'd expected to find junk piled everywhere: paint cans, old bikes, broken furniture, plenty of hiding spots to choose from. It was a basement, after all. But Anne Sager had other ideas. He saw one small desk with a brass lamp, one ladder-back chair, one large, immovable metal file cabinet, and a side-by-side washer-dryer. Even if he was willing to suffer the indignity of curling up inside the dryer, he'd never be able to climb out in time. His best bet was to hide underneath the Bilco door stairs, despite the fact they had no back, no risers between the treads. He'd be visible.

A half hour passed. Coigne's joints ached. He also wondered about black mold. Worst of all, he'd begun to think they'd set their trap for nothing. Singh was probably miles away and they were wasting time. If by some miracle they caught Singh, he was only good for the murder of Ken Crawford and Gin Sager. Not even kryptonite could weaken his alibi for Buddy Todd's time of death. But for Coigne, doubtful and discouraged were foreign states of mind. His hunches generally bore out. He stopped second-guessing and settled in for a long wait.

To pass the time he thought about Norma's odd behavior ever since Laney's rescue at the high school. He wondered if she still thought he took bribes from crooks. The notion of having to plead his case to convince her otherwise didn't sit well. He needed her to figure out who he was by herself. To be fair, he knew why she thought he was a dirty cop. After all, his father was a convicted criminal. What she didn't know was the dirty-cop rumors were started by his father, retribution for Coigne's crossing to the "dark side," law enforcement. Coigne figured he'd get over the hurt his father had inflicted once he got a little retribution of his own, when he could inform his father that attempted bribery, a consequence of his father's dirty-cop rumor, just added two years to the sentence of a guy who had tried it on him.

An hour and a half had passed and judging by the color of the sky and stiffness of his joints, it would be evening soon. They'd told Ferguson to bring Anne back in two hours, at which time, if Singh hadn't appeared, Coigne would reconnoiter with Katepoo and work on Plan B.

Despite his facility for tying loose ends into tidy knots, something was still eating him, something he'd forgotten. He went over and over the plan and could find nothing wrong. It took just three small words from the floor above to jog his memory.

"Gran, you home?"

42

Coigne held his breath. My God, what was Laney doing back so soon? He pulled out his cell phone to contact Katepoo. No service. Stupid! He started to uncoil his limbs when, overhead, the Bilco hinges groaned. Daylight poured in. The Bilco doors closed. A pair of dark pants crept backwards down the ladder stairs. *Singh.*

"Gran? Where are you? You'll never guess what I saw!"

Singh stopped mid-step.

Coigne thrust his hands through the open stairs and grabbed Singh's ankles. He yanked hard. Singh fell back, head first, hitting concrete. Coigne squeezed out from under the stairs and drew his gun. Singh rolled over and whirled around. He stood in shadow but his white sleeve was caught in the light. A click sound drew Coigne's attention to the open switchblade.

The men faced off. For a wild second, Coigne thought of the show on stage at the Academy, *West Side Story*. But there was no Bernstein score for courage, no fellow gang members. Just an armed killer and cop in a laundry room.

"Gran?"

Singh made as if to raise his hands in surrender, grabbed the brass lamp and flung it at Coigne's head, causing him to drop his gun.

Coigne shouted, "Run, Laney! Get out of the house!"

Singh scrambled toward the stairs to the kitchen. *Where the hell was Katepoo?* Singh bolted up the stairs two at a time. His fingers reached for the kitchen doorknob. Coigne lunged for his legs. Missed. The door swung open full force, flipping Singh over Coigne and landing him flat on his back.

"Drop the knife. I said drop it." Jimmy Katepoo stood ten feet tall at the top of the stairs, gun drawn.

"Where's Gran? Is my Gran okay?" Laney was ghost white. Handing Singh over to Katepoo for the Miranda warning, Coigne led the girl into the living room. He was getting her a glass of water when Trooper Ferguson and Anne Sager returned to the house. Coigne knew Ms. Sager would be furious that her granddaughter had been caught in the trap laid for Singh. Who wouldn't be? He was relieved when he saw that getting Laney up to bed was her grandmother's first priority.

To Katepoo he said, "Put that piece of crap in my car. We'll take him in together. And Jimmy, damn good work."

"Glad you had me stay outside. You really did think of everything."

"If you only knew."

43

Katepoo talked to Barb Ferguson in the Sagers' yard while Coigne called ahead to the district court where Singh would be placed in lock-up and booked. He got another call the moment he hung up.

"Got your voicemail, Coigne. And yes, use my driveway. You didn't need to wait for my permission."

"Glad to hear you say that, Norma. We didn't wait. Look, can I call you back? We're taking Singh in right now."

"You got him."

"Yep. In the back seat. Details later." He hated to hang up. He looked forward to telling her about it, watching her face as he walked her through each step. If only he could skip the part about failing to anticipate Laney's early return. The girl could have been kidnapped again, or killed. Even if he tried to hide that part from Norma, foolish though that would be, Anne Sager would tell her all about it. Coigne adjusted his rearview mirror so he could see Singh's face. "You comfortable back there?"

"Quite comfortable. And you?"

"Never better. Enjoy your cushy seat, because they've never heard of upholstery where you're headed."

"By contrast, I hear you know quite a bit about the soft life."

"What're you talking about?"

Katepoo called over to Coigne. "Be with you in a minute."

Singh spoke quickly. "You've been known to accept consideration in return for helping people in my situation. Am I right?"

"If you're saying what I think you're saying, just hold on."

"I think ten grand should cover the cost of an unfortunate car accident that would allow me to escape, and your partner unfortunately would have to—"

Coigne nodded toward Katepoo, who was heading toward the cruiser. "I don't cut my partner out. Wait until he gets in."

The young trooper looked in the backseat before getting in. Coigne detected the smile beneath his solemn face.

"Now continue, Mr. Singh," Coigne said, pulling out of Norma's driveway.

"I was saying ten grand should cover the cost of an accident permitting me to escape."

"Yes, right, and once you take off we get paid how?" Katepoo said.

"You have heard of Tissot?"

"Who's that?" Coigne asked.

"It is not a *who*, it is a watch, Lieutenant. My watch, to be precise."

"I saw it. Nice watch. So what?"

"Each hour is diamond-studded. That's two carats, ten thousand dollars. The watch is worth at least that."

"Time really *is* precious. Hand it over. Let me see." Katepoo reached for the watch.

"No. Not until the accident.

Coigne said, "It's a deal. Trooper Katepoo, we head toward the courthouse. I know a good place for an accident." To Singh he said, "Be about thirty minutes this time of day."

"You're the boss."

From time to time as they drove, Coigne caught Singh watching him in the rear view mirror, waiting for a signal the accident was about to occur.

Forty minutes later they arrived at the courthouse, a modest, pale orange building, part brick, part concrete. Singh struggled to get out of his seat, his face a battlefield between fear and hatred. "What're we doing here?"

Coigne turned around. "Taking you in, barfbag. What does it look like?"

Katepoo got out. "I'll get the evidence bag from the trunk."

Coigne nodded. Two troopers came out of the building and headed their way. Katepoo waved.

Coigne turned to the backseat. "And you get to keep your Tissot, Mr. Singh—for about five more minutes."

Katepoo opened the back door and pulled Singh out. "I sure could have used a new watch."

"I could have paid off my car with that cash," Coigne said, joining the group as they escorted their prisoner inside.

"Coigne! Coigne! What's going on there? You left your cell phone on, moron. I heard the whole thing. Hell. I'm coming down there."

44

"I'm too old for this."

"We're just going for a drive, Norma. Simmer down," Coigne said.

She had arrived at the courthouse and sat in the parking lot for what seemed like hours. Her initial impulse was to barge in and get a good look at the piece of shit responsible for terrorizing Laney. She didn't do it. This was Coigne's show.

Coigne had finally walked out of the building with a five o'clock shadow and baggy eyes, but his slow smile in Norma's direction hinted he was satisfied. He told her he'd answer all her questions about Singh's arrest, but only once they were on the road. He needed to drive. They'd pick up her car later.

"Why do we have to go for a drive for you to answer my questions?"

"Let's just say we're mixing business and pleasure."

She got in and slammed the cruiser door. "I don't do pleasure drives. I'm too old for that."

As if only now considering the question, he asked, "How old are you anyway?"

"Thirty-nine."

"You're lying."

"Jerk."

They drove down the Mid-Cape Highway in silence. Norma wondered where they were headed but was reluctant to ask. She didn't want to belabor the pleasure drive-discomfort issue. It made her seem unsophisticated. How she appeared to others didn't usually bother her. She tried to relax. "Why didn't you tell me the rumors about your being on the take were false?"

He didn't answer.

"I said—"

"I heard you. I was trying to think of a truthful answer. I guess I wanted you to figure it out on your own. I was hoping you knew me well enough to realize the rumors couldn't be true."

"How could I realize it in the face of all the evidence to the contrary?"

"Evidence. That's just it. I wanted you to think like a human, not a lawyer."

"The two being mutually exclusive, of course."

"Besides, if I'd told you the truth and you didn't believe me, where would that leave us?"

"Us? What 'us'?"

The cruiser entered the brand new rotary. It was said the rotary's construction had suffered steep budget cuts, up to fifty percent, so its circumference was fifty percent what it should have been. The local paper called it "tight as a panty girdle." The third exit led toward the beach where the Pilgrims set eyes on Native Americans for the first time.

Norma said, "It's an incredible coincidence the Pilgrims landed on a beach called First Encounter Beach? Okay, dumb joke."

He smiled.

She suspected he was heading to Fort Trent. No matter what time of year, she loved hiking through the park's forests and fields and exploring the salt marshes. But she loved it when she was alone. Right now she felt only turmoil. She decided the only thing to do was to say what was on her mind. "I'm sorry I didn't see through the bribery thing sooner, Coigne. I did figure out something, though."

"Shoot."

But she couldn't say more. It would be like leaping blindfolded over quicksand. Instead, she hummed nervously.

"You were saying, Norma? You figured out what?"

"I figured out where we're going. Fort Trent. Do you know there's a huge rock on one of the trails Native Americans used to sharpen tools? There's even a special groove where the tribe's shrew sharpened her tongue. Please, no obvious comment about my familiarity with that groove." She forced a laugh. Its heartiness amplified his silence.

"We should call it a day, Coigne. You're exhausted. You can tell me all about catching Singh after a rest."

Coigne answered by steering onto a winding road. It snaked up through high beach grasses on either side, passing an occasional shingled antique, a bed and breakfast, and a graceful old captain's house, tribute to a nineteenth century whaling family. It welcomed tourists through an odd-shaped arch made of whale bone.

They reached the end of the road. "Let's get out," he said.

They stood side by side against a rotting split-rail fence at the crest of the hill. On top of the world, they breathed in Nauset Marsh, Coast Guard Beach, and the Atlantic Ocean. Sunrise cast a balm over fields of wildflowers sloping down to the beach. To the west, a lone kayaker paddled through a canal. Without warning, a breeze whipped Norma's skirt into a frenzy and she bent over to hold it down with both hands. "Ha! Do I look like Marilyn Monroe caught over a street vent?"

The breeze died. Coigne's eyes remained fixed on the horizon.

She turned away from Coigne and straightened up. "What I really meant before, when I said there was something I'd figured out, was this. It didn't matter to me whether or not you took bribes. I liked you anyway."

Her confession mortified her. He'd think she was so desperate for a late-in-life, now-or-never fling she was willing to abandon all moral sense. Maybe she was, but she wished she'd kept it to herself. She'd spoken softly and now hoped the wind had carried off her momentary madness. Coigne was quiet and he seemed lost in thought. She was beginning to feel optimistic. Maybe he hadn't heard her.

He took her hand. Another breeze lifted her skirt. It billowed wildly. She struggled to control it with her free hand, then let go.

45

Sunrise on the Cape was an early morning opera. The birds tuned up at 4:00 a.m., and by 4:05 were well into their overture. Norma was awake anyway. She stood in front of her bathroom mirror examining her face for signs that the evening before with Coigne had changed it. She felt like someone else. Surely that showed. But it was the same strong jaw and slight overbite. She leaned in closer. She saw a woman trying hard not to laugh.

As a concession to Coigne's comment the night before— "You've got style, Norma"—she took five minutes instead of three to dress. The skirt from yesterday would do, her lucky skirt.

Ravenous with hunger, she headed to the kitchen. In that room no one would ever suspect it was the 21st century: no individual coffee maker, no soapstone countertop, and no double-bowl stainless steel sink. Mr. Coffee and Formica counters worked fine, though her sink could use some Ajax. She spread peanut butter on toast, shook bacon-bits and raisins on top, and crunched her way to the front porch.

By now the birds had gotten the surprise of sunrise out of their systems. When she'd first moved to the cottage, they would all flock to a ledge on her porch, an ideal spot for nesting as evidenced by the wisps of cotton strands and bird droppings everywhere. Instead of moving the ledge, Norma fortified it with two-by-fours to contain spillage. Now warblers swooped from across the yard and landed, displacing their angered kin, who'd fly off and whistle protest folk songs.

Norma suspected her preoccupation this morning with birds was tied somehow to yesterday's events, but it also allowed her to delay thinking about Anne. The conversation she needed to have would be awkward. "Needed to have" because Laney's safety was still at risk. Sure, Varn was dead and Singh, locked up, but as Coigne had warned, Singh had a boss, and the missing letter was still that, missing.

The question was how to approach Anne? Why should it be so difficult? They were best friends. Norma knew most people saw her as loud and rash, as did Anne. But her friend not only didn't mind these traits, she delighted in them.

"You're the person I would have been if I'd had more courage, less refinement. You're my *id*, Norma."

"I think you mean *idiot*, but never mind."

Anne was not easily led to divulging information unless she meant to. She would immediately catch on if she were being manipulated by Norma into spilling the beans, and close down. Worse, she'd retain the bitter aftertaste of such a ploy.

The logical answer was to approach Anne directly, but how could she? It was none of Norma's business, and by asking she'd make a fool of herself. She almost wished Dohnan hadn't unwittingly tipped her off.

Her hesitation concerned her. *Have I turned myself into a ninny with my Coigne crush? Oh well, 'Twere well it were done quickly.*

Anne's car was parked in her driveway, but no one answered the door. Norma stepped inside.

"Knock, knock. Hello, hello. Anne?"

Anne appeared from the back hall. Her hair was flattened on one side. Her slacks, normally pressed, were wrinkled and her top, untucked. She squinted, as though even early-morning sun was too bright.

"Looks like you slept in your clothes. You must be absolutely exhausted, poor woman. Did I wake you?"

"Good morning, Norma." Anne came into the living room and leaned against a wall, arms folded.

"Your usual greeting is a kiss on the cheek or a shoulder squeeze. I've lost my touch," Norma said. "Anyway, thought I'd stop by and see how you're doing after all the hubbub yesterday. Coigne told me about Singh's arrest. Awful for Laney. For both of you. Is she here?"

"No."

Norma waited, but Anne didn't elaborate. Anne's clipped answer probably meant she wanted Norma to shove off so she could get back to bed. Norma sat down. "I was wondering. It's a small detail, need to clear it up."

"I see something's on your mind, but can it wait? I'm awfully tired."

"No. I'm sorry, Anne. It can't."

Anne shrugged and joined Norma by the couch, but didn't sit down. "What is it?"

"I'm wondering," Norma said, fiddling with the fringe on a throw pillow "why you're getting legal advice from Bitty Buchanan. Have I done something wrong? You know she's unethical, don't you? She thinks a scruple is a German pastry."

Anne cracked a smile. "Don't tell me you're jealous."

Norma laughed, like they were having a good joke. "It's not jealousy. It's that I had to learn about it from this other lawyer, Derek Dohnan. It was a tad humiliating."

"You know I'm grateful for your legal advice, Norma. For all your help. God—you can't possibly doubt that?"

"Okay, I'm great. Now how about it? Why Bitty? She's a divorce lawyer. You're a widow."

"You're right. Ms. Buchanan doesn't have a stellar reputation. But she knows family law. That's what she does. You're a generalist, Norma, as you've told me many times. And you're an excellent one. Besides, I was, well, you know it was just an impulse."

As Anne mentioned "family law," another conversation with Anne came back to Norma. What had Anne said?

Norma's momentary distraction allowed Anne to go on. "I had a few questions about my role as Laney's legal guardian, that's all." In a slightly mocking tone she said, "I'm completely loyal to you, Norma, and I'll never consult her again. Scouts honor." She saluted. "Better?" Anne wandered to the window by her piano.

Norma had seen Anne mock other people, but always when they deserved it and with such a light touch they only suspected ill-will. She and Anne would later snicker as the target tried to work it out. Now Norma was the target. She tossed the pillow away and waited until Anne rejoined her.

"Did you consult Bitty because there was something you didn't want me to know?"

"I've just told you why I consulted her, Norma. What's making you so insecure anyway? Did that lieutenant put you up to this? By the way, you said he was dirty, but the other evening you sure seemed to have warmed to him."

It was as Norma feared. Anne was trying to change the subject. Coigne. What about Coigne? Then it came to her. It had been a casual remark during that awful meeting with Coigne about the cigarette pack and Rahul Singh. Anne had said something about Laney's father and paternity claims. Anne must have talked to Bitty Buchanan about Buddy Todd's paternity claims. Why else do you go to a family lawyer? But what paternity claims? Norma regarded her friend, who seemed tired and oblivious to the tension in the room. Norma was about to raise it up a notch for her.

"Did you already know Buddy was in town before he rolled up on the beach, dead?"

Anne didn't hesitate. "I did, actually. He came to see me. Said he wanted custody of Laney. Incredible. I sent him packing. But if you're going to throw the book at me for not sharing this detail with you and the authorities, even though maybe I should have…maybe there was a reasonable argument to be made—"

"Like Laney's life was at stake!" Norma picked up the pillow and hurled it across the room.

"Wait a minute. Do you think if I'd known there was any connection between Laney's kidnapping and Buddy's bothersome visit I wouldn't have shared every detail with the police? But I didn't. You're looking at the situation with 20/20 hindsight. The last thing I wanted, the last thing that was in Laney's interest when she went missing, was to get the police off on a wild goose chase about Buddy's visit."

"Bullshit, Anne. There was a whole day between the discovery of the body on the beach and Laney's disappearance. You could have sped up the identification of his body by coming forward sooner. Everyone in the neighborhood was asked if any stranger had been around. If you'd spoken up, everything might have changed." Norma was shouting.

Except for a slight pallor, Anne didn't appear shaken by Norma's tirade. "I had no idea it was Buddy who'd drowned and rolled up on the beach. I am telling you the truth—I had repressed that man's previous visit."

"At some point, Anne, you must have realized there was a connection between his demand for custody and Gin's, and Ken Crawford's murder, and most of all, Laney's kidnapping. And even if you didn't, that's the goddamn reason for the goddamn rule that you tell the police everything you know and let them put it together. You're not a dummy, Anne. You know that."

After a long silence, Anne nodded. Her voice shook as she said, "I know it now. I made a horrible mistake." She seemed to wilt.

Their argument was leading nowhere. And how was it that, in a few short minutes, years of trust and friendship had gotten blown to smithereens? Norma knew she'd be devastated once she had time to reckon with all she'd just lost. For now, she needed answers. There was no longer any mystery about what all the bad guys had been after. She just couldn't figure out how it all had gotten started and who killed Buddy. Other than Anne, who now seemed too tired to be helpful, everyone who could possibly enlighten her, Gin, Buddy, Old Man Todd, and Ken Crawford, was dead. She had only one card to play.

46

On her way to Bitty Buchanan's office, Norma considered a call to Lieutenant Coigne, but hesitated. She relived the scene she'd just had with Anne. She'd had no right to scold her best friend and by telling Coigne about Anne's visit from Buddy Todd, she would be subjecting her to another angry grilling, this time by the police.

On the other hand, Norma had excoriated Coigne for holding back information from her. Wouldn't she be guilty of the same if she didn't call him?

She wished she didn't agonize over these quandaries. No one else did. She resolved the problem by making the appointment with Bitty her priority. After all, Bitty's secretary, Donna, said she'd have to be leaving for court promptly at 11:00. Norma would catch up with Coigne afterwards, when she would have even more to tell him.

Donna greeted Norma. She was a contented girl whose large, sleepy eyes and gently shifting jaw brought to mind a camel chewing gum. The walls of the reception area were covered in framed photos and headlines touting Bitty's triumphs. One photo in particular caught Norma's eye. Bitty was celebrating her election as president of the bar. She was standing arm in arm with other trial attorneys, all male, on a fishing boat. The caption read: "President Buchanan enjoys swimming with the sharks!"

"Yes, and that's not all she's doing with them," Norma said to herself. She wasn't really shocked that Bitty had slept her way to the top, and to the top it was. Another more recent headline read, "Buchanan Throws Hat in Ring for Judgeship." It didn't even bother her that Bitty represented lowlifes in nasty divorce matters. In one case, "nasty" meant the ex-husband had strangled his wife. To hide the evidence, he decapitated her. No photo with *that* article. What bothered Norma was Bitty's bad taste, in décor, fashion, and men. "Derek Dohnan? I rest my case."

"What brings you to my neighborhood, Norma?" Bitty swanned into the reception area with hand extended, head tilted back for a sleeker neckline. To Norma's eye, the ambush impact of Bitty's in-your-face cleavage was outgunned by her shoes, five-inch heels with black leather straps laced up her calves.

"God, Bitty. Where'd you get those slave sandals, the Colosseum?"

Bitty smiled, forgivingly. "Do come in, Norma."

"You look like Ben-Hur, dressed for success."

"You're so funny. This way."

"Ah. The lion's den." Norma waved to Donna as she followed the bouncing ball of Bitty's booty.

"Make yourself at home." Bitty motioned her to sit down.

Norma looked around.

"Like it?"

Bitty had carried the decorating scheme from her reception area, "All about Me and My Success," into her office. Everywhere you looked was a mirror or reflecting glass, and the few remaining blank spaces were filled with more news clips of Bitty's victories. Norma noticed a picture of Bitty sharing a toast with a rough gangster type— unshaven, scowling, dark sunglasses, expensive suit. According to the caption, they were in an exotic hotel for the superrich. The gangster was surrounded by his toughs and there was a champagne fountain in the foreground. The toughs looked like they could really use a glass. Her eyes on the photo, she thought she could use one, too.

Norma said, "It's great. And I'm stunned by the scope of your practice." She nodded toward the gangster photo. "But that's for another day. I know you're due in court, so I'll forge ahead."

"Please do."

"I'm assisting the police with some loose ends in their investigation of Buddy Todd's murder. Now, Todd's daughter's grandmother, Anne Sager, is your client." Norma hesitated, unsure of how to ease into her request. "You've heard about her troubles. It's all over the news."

"I'm just glad her granddaughter was found and they caught the kidnapper." Bitty shifted a pile of documents already neatly stacked on her desk.

"Right. I'm here about a different matter. It's awkward, but I need to know what Anne consulted you about."

"Really, Norma. I know she's your client, too. I didn't poach, you know. I have no need, obviously." Bitty looked sideways at her reflection in the wall mirror and smiled.

As Norma explained her role in the police investigation, hoping to convince Bitty to open up, Bitty pulled an emery board from her desk drawer and gave some attention to Mr. Pinky.

Norma persevered. "Anne's consultation with you may help the police determine—"

"Don't you really think you should be talking to Anne?"

"I did already, you numbskull. Why else would I be here?" Norma said to herself.

"As a matter of fact, Norma, Anne called before you arrived." Bitty again reached into her desk, for nail polish—Deluscious Lollipop. "She said you might contact me. I was instructed not to discuss her affairs with you." Bitty had unscrewed the cap and was wiping excess polish off the brush tip. "Anne seemed to think I needed a refresher course on my professional responsibilities. I explained I would never breach the attorney-client privilege by speaking with you about her private matters. I found the implication that I might quite offensive. I hope you had nothing to do with that." Bitty held up her hand for a good, long look at her achievement. Then, "If that's all?"

"Almost."

Something wasn't right. Bitty's hand, when she held it up, was shaking. That was not in character at all. And that privilege lecture? Bitty didn't want to talk about Anne, but it wasn't because of professional responsibilities. Norma had to find out what was behind that reluctance. Time to be bad.

"I'm in total agreement with you, Bitty. It is vitally important to protect our clients' confidences and secrets."

Bitty nodded, pleased with teacher's pet.

"Of course, *you're* not *my* client, Bitty. I don't have to keep *your* secret."

"And what secret would that be?"

"It's not such an exceptional secret. Trite, in fact. What's important is who would care to know the secret."

"Who?" Bitty's smile began to slip.

"Linda Dohnan, for one. You know, wife of Derek Dohnan for twenty years, bearer of four little Dohnanettes."

"I don't know what—"

"You're right. Linda won't care. She'll jump for joy to be relieved of her wifely duties to that mouth-foaming pig. On the other hand, did I hear you've decided to run for judge and expect to be endorsed by the bar? I'm sure they'd like to know—"

"You wouldn't dare." Bitty looked ready to break a few nails across Norma's face.

Norma placed her thumbs together like a frame. "Picture those headlines, honey." She rose and got as far as the door.

"Wait."

Norma stopped but kept her hand on the doorknob.

"I can't tell you what Anne wanted. You know I can't, Norma. Believe it or not, I do have ethics."

"Screwing someone else's husband certainly supports that claim."

"Sit down, Norma, for God's sake. Please." In the last sixty seconds, Bitty's face had lost all color and luster. Even Mr. Pinky looked pale.

"It wasn't the nature of the advice Anne sought that was unusual," Bitty explained. "I think you can figure out why laws on custody interested her, especially since she dotes on that grandkid and Buddy Todd wanted her back. And by the way, I'm not violating the privilege by merely stating the law: Natural parents are always going to have priority over a grandparent in a custody dispute, all other things being equal."

Norma knew the law, and Anne had already told her Buddy Todd wanted custody of Laney. "Go on, Bitty. You say that's what I can figure out. Now what is it I can't figure out?"

"Anne wanted me to contact someone for her. I can't tell you who and I can't tell you why. And you'll never figure it out. Even the judgeship isn't worth my telling you, so don't push." Bitty crossed her arms, a note of triumph creeping back into her voice.

But Bitty was wrong. Norma did figure it out and it broke her heart.

47

Norma feared she'd be too late. She'd been blind from the start, but never before with such dire consequences. She'd failed to interpret her best friend's disheveled clothes and uncombed hair. As always, she'd been too wrapped up in her own agenda.

That Anne had killed Buddy Todd was the only scenario that made sense. Norma even understood why, fear for Laney. But Bitty's disclosure that Anne needed a contact meant only one thing, and that one thing outdistanced the farthest reaches of Norma's imagination. How could Anne do it? Enlightenment came while she sat in Bitty's parking lot. It left her paralyzed when she should have been rushing back to Anne.

The envelope with Norma's name was propped against Anne's bedside lamp. Norma sat beside her on the bed, held her limp, pulseless wrist and smoothed her baby soft hair away from her face. This way, when the first responders arrived, they'd see Anne's beauty, intelligence, and goodness even in death.

Norma was tempted to shred the letter without reading it. Better not to know for sure. But her thoughts were on Laney. She didn't even know where Laney was and hoped the letter would tell her. She had five minutes before others arrived.

Dear Norma,

I know you will determine the right thing to do once you read this letter. As bumbling and awkward as you think you are, you've always been able to figure out right from wrong and act accordingly. I may have had that same ability at one time.

To set a course of action, you'll need to know everything, though you've probably pieced it together by now.

Buddy came to see me and, like I said, demanded custody of Laney. Can you believe it, at this late date? After all his trips to rehab? He expected to take her with him when he left the Cape in a few days and I was to have her ready. Gin would side with him, he said. He'd gotten in touch with her about Old Man Todd's bequest. He had the infamous letter that proved Old Man Todd intended the beach access property for Laney but had been swindled out of it. Buddy said they'd be wealthy and Laney would be better off with her natural parents anyway, and why he'd ever agreed to allow me to raise Laney in the first place he didn't know. I thought he was high, the way he was spewing nonsense, but decided to check out his claims by talking to the toughest family law attorney in the state, according to the Internet reviews.

Norma thought of Bitty and could guess who wrote the reviews.

You can imagine how I felt when I learned that degenerate might actually win custody, or maybe you can't. What I didn't tell you about Buddy when you asked why I never told you about him is that he tried to sell Laney. Yes, like a used bike. When Laney was three, he tried to exchange her for a bag—that is, one dose of heroin. But for the interference of a nosey old woman, a neighbor, who spied Laney in the back alley with a stranger, kicking and crying for her mother, he would have gotten away with it. By the time I learned of all this, Buddy was in jail for something else. I couldn't prove any of it had happened.

Ms. Buchanan convinced me that if Buddy were clean and persuaded Gin to join him in the custody battle, he stood a reasonable chance. The rights of the natural parents are second only to the best interests of the child.

I'd rather die than leave Laney in his care and told

him so the next time he came. Surprisingly, the fool was prepared with an answer. He tried to blackmail me. He trotted out a theory I'd murdered my own husband. It wasn't true. I knew Gordon through and through and had he been conscious during those final days, he would have begged me to euthanize him. How Buddy got the notion I'd increased his meds when Gordon's own oncologist suspected nothing, I don't know. Gin must have said something that got him thinking. Whatever Gin suspected, she never mentioned it to me. But it wouldn't have mattered if Buddy had gone to the police. No one would have believed him. An autopsy was out of the question since Gordon had been cremated.

So why did I kill Buddy? I realized it wasn't that I'd rather die than see him take Laney, it was that I'd rather he die. And he'd just given me the opportunity to do it. When he arrived to get Laney—the night you took her to the ball game and kept her overnight—he came on foot, so there was no car to dispose of. He had no friends, no contacts on the Cape. If he'd told anyone he was coming to see me, I'd have had a story ready as to how he was fine when he left. The sod had even put into my mind Gordon's old meds. Your pal, Lieutenant Coigne, knows Buddy was drugged. If you choose to go this way, you can tell him Buddy was out long enough for me to bind him in duct tape—I had it handy from repairing Gin's tail light over a year ago—and haul him down to the beach in Cockle Cove. When there's no moon, it's pitch black at 2:00 a.m. I dragged him onto someone's beached dory and rowed him pretty far out. He weighed a ton but I was desperate and that gave me near-Herculean strength. But taking him there was my first mistake, forgetting that the tide flows north. It brought him right back to our doorstep on Samoset Beach, where Laney found him. I told you earlier today I had no idea it was Buddy's body Laney found on the beach and that is the truth. I had so dissociated myself from what I'd done that I was shocked when Coigne told us it was Buddy.

Norma heard a siren in the distance but kept reading.

The letter wasn't on Buddy when he came that second time. He said he'd hidden it. I had to find and destroy it. You're the only one who will believe that I was not interested in the wealth it represented. I knew that if Gin ever found the letter, she'd pull the same stunt as Buddy and try to get Laney back. She tried anyway, even without the letter in hand. But she obviously knew about it.

I asked Ms. Buchanan for the name of someone who could help me, a private investigator maybe, who would stop at nothing to find that letter. She said she knew someone, if I didn't mind engaging a guy from out of town. She said, "Way out of town." She conveyed my instructions for me. What I didn't know, and how could I, was that the contact would take my instructions literally. He kidnapped Laney, thinking she'd lead him to the letter.

I didn't suspect Bitty's out-of-town contact was the kidnapper, Rahul Singh, until I examined that imported pack of cigarettes that Laney found on the beach and we talked to Coigne. Even then, I couldn't be sure.

There it was, confirmation of Norma's worst fears. As soon as she'd seen Rahul Singh's face among the toughs in the hotel fountain photo in Bitty's office, she'd suspected there was a connection between Anne and Singh that predated the kidnapping. It was incomprehensible. Anne had risked Laney's life, exposed her to naked savagery, and indirectly killed her own daughter. Anne knew why Laney had been kidnapped and even by whom, and yet had not come forward.

After our meeting with Coigne when he gave us Singh's name, I contacted Ms. Buchanan immediately and she admitted Rahul Singh was her contact. I told her to have Singh stop his search and release Laney immediately. She got back to me and said he was now working for himself; he had a business interest in finding the letter. Singh had as much financial interest in destroying that letter as Buddy had in preserving it. Singh told her if I said anything to the police about what I knew, Laney would be tortured and dumped on the beach. I know you're judging me, Norma, but I was terrified for Laney.

I am sorry for the long-windedness. I'm coming to a close. Laney is safe now, at least from Rahul Singh. I am not. Even if you don't go to the police, Ms. Buchanan may, although she'd be implicating herself. Or Singh may try to "cop a plea" and "spill his guts" as they say. Or you will figure it out—you almost did—and you may fight your conscience, but you'll end up going to Coigne. One way or another, there will be a sensational trial and Laney will find out my role in her kidnapping and her mother's death. She'll have to live with the certainty each member of her family was a criminal, including me. Most of all, me. She'll never forgive me, and I can't face that.

I'm now doing what I should have done in the first place. I'm asking you to find that letter. I'm also asking you to take care of Laney. My own will asks that you be granted legal guardianship. She's staying overnight with Isabella Miller. Please tell Laney my death was accidental. She may believe it until she's old enough to handle the truth.

My only hope for getting your cooperation is that you love Laney too, and will shield her from pain as I would.

From here to eternity, you are my best friend-

Anne

48

Laney stood on a kitchen chair, Norma close by, and strung colored lights around the top of the Christmas tree. Earlier they'd dragged the tree into the alcove, fit it into its stand, and tethered it to the wall. It was now visible to beach strollers below and made a cheerful contrast to an otherwise foggy Christmas Eve.

"Cheerful contrast" had been Norma's mental mantra throughout the fall. Laney would withdraw for long spells and Norma worried she'd sink into a debilitating depression. A bright smile and gentle squeeze of the girl's shoulder was usually the best Norma could do to signal there were brighter days ahead. She'd learned that Laney's quick nod in response meant she'd gotten the message.

Others tried to help Laney through her cascade of losses. Isabella Miller remained her good friend, and because she was one of the cool kids, she could ward off ignorant and nasty gossip surrounding Laney that fall. Coach Cummings introduced her to gymnastics. She got good at it and even became something of a school phenomenon, for reasons other than her role in the summer's drama.

Coigne was a regular at music performances and sporting events, and for that matter, at dinnertime. It rattled Norma that Laney sometimes turned to him for propping up and advice, but she was also grateful Coigne was there to help.

Norma tried to satisfy Anne's last wishes. She destroyed her suicide note before anyone arrived, reasoning, *after all, what are best friends for?* When she told Laney her Gran's death was an accident, Laney never challenged the characterization, which proved there are some things you believe because you have to. The DA's office was too busy prosecuting Derek Dohnan for swindling Old Man Todd and having Norma assaulted, her home trashed, and her dog killed, to worry about tagging a dead woman with Buddy's murder. They were happy to let any lingering odor from Buddy's "unsolved" murder linger over Dohnan and his sidekick, Bitty "the Broker" Booty Buchanan, "broker" because she had negotiated a nice fee from Dohnan for connecting him to Rahul Singh and Lancelot Varn, whom Dohnan hired to attack Norma. She'd probably extracted a similar fee from Anne for hiring Singh to find the Old Man Todd letter, but Norma saw no reason to bring that up as Bitty was going down as it was.

As for the Temple brothers, they were implicated in the swindle of Old Man Todd, but no charges were ever brought against them. Just as well, as they were fighting insurance fraud charges when, conveniently during the off-season, the Inn at Cockle Cove burned to a crisp.

She'd not been able to deliver on Anne's other request, to find the letter. Even though anyone interested in it was in prison or dead, Norma knew Laney could become someone's prey so long as the letter might resurface. There were plenty of thugs in Bitty's hotel photo.

In her suicide note, Anne had said Buddy didn't have the letter with him during his second visit, that he'd hidden it. Norma retraced his steps between his two visits. All indications were that Buddy went nowhere other than his room at the Skaket Seaside Hotel, which had been torn apart during the murder investigation. According to Coigne, even the bed bugs got strip-searched. She figured Buddy must have mailed the letter to someone for safekeeping, except there was no evidence he'd bought stamps. She was at a dead end, and could do nothing but worry.

Coigne arrived for dinner carrying a quart of eggnog and a new CD of Christmas carols. Norma judged by the wrapping he'd made his purchases at the minimart. She glanced at the jewel case. "Is there a message here, Coigne?" She read out loud, "Three Celtic Babes for Christmas."

"The guy said they sound like Enya."

Laney looked up from setting the table. "What's Eeen-ya?"

"Nothin's eatin' me. What's eatin' you?" Coigne answered.

Laney groaned.

They sat down to honey-glazed baked ham while "O Holy Night" wailed eerily in the background. Something was up. The way Coigne and Laney kept looking at each other, then looking away, was suspicious.

They finished dessert and Coigne folded his napkin three different ways, placed it on the table and stood. "Will you ladies join me in the living room?"

"What's up?"

"Come on, Aunt Norma. Let's go." Laney was halfway to the living room.

"You know what this is about, Laney?"

"Let's go!" Coigne stood behind her and hoisted her by the armpits.

The CD had ended. Norma and Laney sat side by side on the couch, warmed by the crackling fire and comfortable in their red plaid flannel shirts. Lancy's was tucked in and her hair was coiled on top. Norma's shirt was threadbare and she'd clasped her hair with a chip-bag clip.

Coigne stood before them. He no longer seemed confident, more like a prisoner facing the parole board.

"Now what?" Norma said.

Coigne cleared his throat. "I have something to say."

"It's really neat, Aunt Norma. I hope you'll say yes."

Coigne's eyes shifted from Norma to Laney. "Ahem."

"Quit clearing your damn throat and tell me."

"Coigne inherited a farm in West Virginia and wants us to go with him. To live there, Aunt Norma."

"You're joking."

Silence.

"Coigne?"

"She's right. I've inherited this farmhouse on a hundred acres in the eastern panhandle of West Virginia."

"So sell it."

"There's a big barn with a stable, four paddocks and a view —"

"Are you out of your mind? Are you really thinking of leaving the Cape for a-a-a panhandle?"

"Not without you two."

"Coigne says we could have horses."

"It's nuts."

"Stop shaking your head, Aunt Norma. And which part is nuts, the farm or the marriage proposal?"

More silence.

"I didn't hear a marriage proposal, Laney."

"It didn't come out the way I'd intended." Coigne dropped down on one knee. "Or at the *time* I'd intended." He glared at Laney.

"Oh get up! And where is *West* Virginia? It's not even worthy of having its own name."

"That's dumb, Aunt Norma."

"Let's let her digest the idea, Laney. Come on. Let's get the brochures out of my car."

"There's also this cool college town nearby with a gymnastics program," Laney said on her way out.

Norma tried to look interested in the pictures of mountains, rivers, and covered bridges they spread before her, but it was all a blur. Coigne's impulse to move to a foreign country, practically, was lunacy. What about his job? Her job? She wasn't licensed to practice law in West Virginia. Did they have laws in West Virginia? And Laney? What was she so excited about, leaving everything she'd ever known? The icing on the cake, a *marriage* proposal. Jee-sus.

She looked over at Coigne and Laney, their heads together, poring over some annual film festival brochure. She didn't want to spoil their fun. It was Christmas Eve. Laney was more animated than she'd been in a long time.

"Okay, you two. I'll agree to think over the propositions if you'll agree to table the discussion until after Christmas. For now, let's have some Christmas carols." She looked pointedly at the CD player. "I mean real Christmas carols, not spa music. Laney, let's tickle the ivories."

They'd had Anne's baby grand moved to Norma's house. It made the whole house feel tight, but when Norma had asked Laney what they should do with it, she'd said, "No matter what, Gran loved me. Selling the piano would be like denying that." Norma couldn't argue with that logic.

Coigne cleared away his brochures and walked over to the piano. "It's your funeral. I can't hold a tune and I never remember more than the first stanza of any carol."

"Don't worry. Gran kept some Christmas sheet music in here." Laney lifted the lid of the piano seat and waded through sonatas and etudes and stopped. "What's this? Looks like a letter." She handed Norma an old envelope. Coigne skimmed its contents over Norma's shoulder.

"Well, well, well, what do you make of that, Norma?"

"I'd say Merry Christmas!"

Acknowledgments

I would like to thank Lieutenant Andrew R. Martin, MSP/Ret (Massachusetts State Police/Retired), who gave tirelessly of his time, expertise and wisdom in explaining law enforcement procedures and little known details about the criminal investigative process on the Cape. Special thanks are also owed to two very competent and busy lawyers, Kathleen E. Kilkenny and Daniel L. Kilkenny, for explaining some of the real estate and corporate law concepts that crop up in *Tidal Kin*. Any errors pertaining to the law or law enforcement in *Tidal Kin* are entirely my own. I also want to thank my readers, Janice E. Strobl, and Mary D. McCarthy, both book lovers, who bravely pointed out errors and generously provided encouragement. Rising Tide Writers, my writing group, deserves a week in the Bahamas for providing me with insightful guidance along the way. And last but never least, I want to thank Julia Gabis and the superb lawyers and staff at 401 East Elm Alliance, who have sat through my readings at our office retreats and supported my writing efforts for many years.